# Murder in the Secret Cold Case

A Mallory Beck Cozy Culinary Caper (Book 7)

Denise Jaden

Denise Jaden Books

# Copyright

# Join my mystery readers' newsletter today!

SIGN UP NOW, AND you'll get access to a special mystery to accompany this series—an exclusive bonus for newsletter subscribers. In addition, you'll be the first to hear about new releases and sales, and receive special excerpts and behind-the-scenes bonuses.

Visit the link below to sign up and receive your bonus mystery:

https://www.subscribepage.com/mysterysignup

# Murder in the Secret Cold Case

A MALLORY BECK COZY Culinary Caper (Book 7)

Spring has arrived in Honeysuckle Grove, and now that crime has finally settled down, Mallory is excited to put her extra time into her new catering business. Despite the lack of crime, though, Alex has been noticeably MIA in Mallory's life, working in the background on a secretive high-profile case. Lately, it's taking up every bit of his time, and it's hard for Mallory not to feel both jilted and curious.

Not meaning to—or at the very least, not completely—Mallory gets a glimpse of detailed clues on Alex's case. The information leaves her breathless, as it quickly becomes clear why Alex has kept this case a secret.

Mallory knows she shouldn't meddle, but at the same time, she can't stay out of this particular investigation, most importantly because she may have key information that will help solve it.

# Contents

1.  Chapter One                    1

2.  Chapter Two                    7

3.  Chapter Three                 15

4.  Chapter Four                  21

5.  Chapter Five                  31

6.  Chapter Six                   35

7.  Chapter Seven                 41

8.  Chapter Eight                 51

9.  Chapter Nine                  54

10.  Chapter Ten                  58

11.  Chapter Eleven               62

12.  Chapter Twelve               66

13.  Chapter Thirteen             68

14.  Chapter Fourteen             73

15.  Chapter Fifteen              76

16.  Chapter Sixteen              81

17.  Chapter Seventeen            85

18.  Chapter Eighteen             91

19.  Chapter Nineteen            100

20.  Chapter Twenty              108

21. Chapter Twenty-one                                             112

22. Chapter Twenty-two                                            115

23. Chapter Twenty-three                                          119

24. Chapter Twenty-four                                           124

25. Chapter Twenty-five                                           128

26. Chapter Twenty-six                                            134

27. Chapter Twenty-seven                                          141

28. Chapter Twenty-eight                                          144

29. Chapter Twenty-nine                                           150

30. Chapter Thirty                                                152

31. Chapter Thirty-one                                            155

32. Chapter Thirty-two                                            160

33. Up Next: Murder in New Orleans...A Mallory        166
    Beck Cozy Culinary Novella (Book 8)

34. Chapter One                                                   167

35. Chapter Two                                                   170

36. Chapter Three                                                 172

37. Reviews Matter...                                             177

From Mallory's Recipe Box – Amber and Mallo-         178
ry's Crepes!

Join My Cozy Mystery Readers' Newsletter To-         181
day!

Acknowledgements                                                 182

# Chapter One

PINK HONEYSUCKLE BLOSSOMS ALWAYS made me feel hopeful, and there was no shortage of the town's namesake in the gardens surrounding the Honeysuckle Grove Community Church. I stopped along the cement pathway from the parking lot and breathed in the sweet fragrance enveloping me on either side.

I was here early to help my friend Sasha set up for this morning's children's church. She would be taking a trip to England in June, and I hoped to learn the ropes to take over for two Sunday mornings. It was too early for the church greeters to be stationed at the doors, so I pulled open the one glass door that had been unlocked and strode into the empty church lobby.

Usually, only a handful of people arrived this early, so it surprised me when I saw a familiar face adjusting pamphlets on the church's bulletin board.

"Amber?" I asked, picking up my pace toward her.

She turned, and her face brightened. Then a second later, her eyes darted to the hallway that led toward the church offices. Tension had been running high in Amber's household for the last few months. Amber's mother and her therapist wanted Amber to spend more time at home and focus on her family, and so according to her mother's new rules, we weren't supposed to be spending time together. Other than a few glances across the worship center at church, I hadn't seen her in almost two months, but Amber's darting eyes made me wonder if her mother was around.

"I was going to ask you first," she said, a note of guilt in her voice. She picked up a letter-sized paper with a color photo of the two of us, along with a mound of food. Without reading any of the text, I could quickly tell this was an ad for our so-far-nameless catering business.

"That looks great, but...?" I trailed off, not quite sure how to ask if this meant her mom was going to allow her to hang out with me and help cater events again. She answered my unasked question.

"I can't do anything else right now, so I figured the least I could do was try and get us some new clients." She shrugged. "As soon as you decide on a location for the food truck, I'll make up flyers for that, too." I'd recently purchased a food truck and spent countless hours cleaning and cooking and acquiring health permits for it, but I still didn't feel confident enough to take it out on my own. "Besides, if someone from the church books us, maybe Mom will rethink letting me at least help with that."

It was a good idea in theory. Unfortunately, we couldn't usually count on logic when it came to Helen Montrose. "How's your mom doing?"

Amber shrugged again. "The same. Hardly goes out. Drugs up on sleeping pills, even during the day sometimes."

"Is she going to drive you around to put up flyers?" Even when I wasn't spending time around Helen Montrose, I felt the need to push her to be a more involved parent to her daughter.

"She'll probably just want to go home after church."

"You know, after Cooper died, I had a brief period where I drove into Bridgeport almost every night because they have a virtual arcade there."

She raised an eyebrow like I wasn't making any sense, and I supposed I wasn't.

"It was good to have a distraction. Healthy for me, I think." Her face didn't change, so I spelled it out for her. "If you need help with things, you should ask your mom. Maybe it would be the distraction she needs."

Amber sighed but didn't respond or look like she agreed with my sentiment.

"Do you want me to put some up around town, too?" I looked down at the stack she had printed off.

She passed me a few but kept most of them for herself. I wouldn't argue. If this was all she could do to help right now, I'd let her have that.

After spending a few minutes making sure everything was okay in her world, I had to rush off to help Sasha. I should have come even earlier if I wanted to have enough time to catch up with my best friend after two months of barely seeing her.

"Sorry I'm late," I called as I opened the counter barrier and entered the main room for the children's church.

Sasha turned with a smile. "No worries. Can you sanitize the toddler toys and post today's Bible study in each room?"

As my seventh-grade teacher, she'd always struck me as a meek woman who could easily be overthrown by her class of twelve-year-olds, but I'd learned since then that her quiet strength was a force to be reckoned with.

"You bet." I placed my purse and the flyers from Amber into a high cubby and then hurried over to the bin of toddler toys.

"The lunch ladies are meeting next Saturday. Can you make it?"

I'd recently started going for lunch with a group of ladies from the church. I was always eager to join them, as the conversation was good and the food at Monica's Café was some of the best I'd had in Honeysuckle Grove. "I was thinking of setting up my food truck Saturday," I told her. "But that can wait."

"Are you sure?" She raised her eyebrows, likely seeing through my insecurities.

"I wouldn't miss a lunch at Monica's."

"Once your food truck is up and running, I'm sure we'll want to lunch there through the summer." She smiled warmly. However long it took me to gain the confidence to set my truck up, I knew I'd at least have a few supporters.

Soon the children started arriving, and I took over with the check-ins. I'd been handling the check-ins and pick-ups more and more, trying to get to know all the parents and kids, along with any allergies or special concerns. I kept busy, and time sped by.

By the time the service ended and all the kids had been picked up, Sasha and I had cleaned up the various children's church rooms. Amber had left long ago, and I had completely forgotten about her flyers until I went to grab my purse.

Sasha looked over my shoulder. "No name yet, huh?"

I shook my head. "Amber's come up with a few good ones, but nothing feels quite right yet."

"Or maybe you're just being overly cautious," Sasha suggested as we flipped up the counter barrier and began to lock up.

It wasn't the first time I'd been tagged with being overly cautious, but that opinion usually came from Amber. "Once we settle on a name, we'll probably keep it for years, so I just want to be sure."

"Of course you do." Sasha's tone was patronizing, but I knew she was only having fun with me. Having her around in the past six months had sharpened me, or at least made me aware of areas I needed to work on in myself. In that way, it was nice having someone a little older in my life. But I also loved the energy and passion that Amber's youth brought.

I had another bout of missing her as Sasha and I walked through the empty church lobby and out to my car. She always got a ride to church with Penny Lismore, the church secretary, but I usually dropped her off when we were done cleaning up.

"No word from Alex lately?" she asked.

I pursed my lips and shook my head.

"I'm sure it's just his heavy caseload that's keeping him away." She placed a gentle hand on my shoulder as we reached my car. Those were the same words I'd been telling myself over and over again about my friend Alex Martinez and his police work, but they rang even less true when Sasha said them. "Once you get your food truck set up and have something else to focus on, I'm sure the time will fly by."

I hoped Sasha's words might be the push I needed, but after dropping her off and going home, I barely had the motivation to make lunch for myself.

I didn't get out and make my way downtown with the flyers until the next morning. Amber had given me five flyers to put up, but it turned out she had already covered most of the downtown core. I wondered if she'd convinced her mom to drive her around to do it yesterday after all. I hoped so.

Eventually, I made my way to the outskirts of town. I put one flyer up at the mini-mart on the way out of town, and the rest at the strip mall near the base of the mountain. After hitting up the nail salon, laundromat, and Mexican restaurant, I paused and looked up at Mayhew Bank.

The bank had been fully rebuilt and renovated since the fire that my husband, Cooper, had died in. Other than closing down our joint account and moving it to the other local bank across town, I had not been inside the building. But Sasha's nudging about my need to move forward with my life was still sitting with me. In an instant, I decided to push myself to be brave and strode for the door.

The bank wasn't terribly large, with three tellers and a couple of offices along a corridor to the left. I strode up to the one available teller, flyer already outstretched. "Hi! I wondered if there was somewhere you'd be able to post this for me?" My voice came out squeaky and strained.

The girl was in her early twenties with a high ponytail and bright pink nails that looked too long to comfortably type with. She looked down at my flyer and took a second to read it over. "You're Mallory Beck?" she asked, looking between my name on the flyer and my face. Her brow furrowed, and so did mine. I guess because our catering business didn't have a name, Amber felt the need to add my personal name to the flyer for the time being. I hadn't thought it was odd until right this second when I saw the strangeness of it on the teller's face.

"That's right." I laughed uncomfortably. "We're a new business and still searching for the perfect name." The adrenaline rush of being inside this bank was starting to rattle me. I slid the flyer another inch toward her. "So can you put it up?"

"I'll have to ask my manager, but probably. Can you leave it with me?"

I smiled my thanks and headed for the door. When I made it back into the fresh spring air, I let out my breath, proud of myself for the first time in a long time. Maybe Helen Montrose wasn't the only one who still needed distractions to overcome her grief and loneliness. I'd come a long way in healing over the last sixteen months, but I still had more to go.

Now, to set an official date to get that food truck on the road.

# Chapter Two

LATER THAT AFTERNOON, I cleaned the extra-large flattop grill in the food truck and tried making crepes on it. They came out thin and delicate with buttery crisp edges. After shutting everything down and cleaning up again, I headed into the house to scour my fridge and cupboards for fun and interesting crepe toppings. As I did that, I made a list and felt my motivation rising.

What would be so hard about opening the food truck downtown one afternoon as a crêperie on wheels? I'd already gotten my business license and a basic health permit, and there weren't a lot of rules governing where I could park it in such a small town. The only thing holding me back at that point was myself.

I texted Amber my idea, and she replied immediately with a screen full of exclamation marks and jumping jack emojis. By that evening, she had sent me a mockup of her newest flyer, baptizing our new business as Amber and Mallory's Crepe Express.

The logo alone was stunning, with what looked like a hand-drawn crepe maker in the middle and both of our names in a beautiful cursive font. I copied, saved it, and sent it off to a local printer to make up a large magnetic sign for both sides of the food truck.

As soon as the signs came in, I'd set a date. This time, I was determined.

I dropped onto the couch beside Hunch later that evening, spent. I hadn't had this full of a day in a long time. Hunch gave me a cursory glance, then laid his head back on his paws and closed his eyes. Hunch missed having company around this house as much as I did. I'd invited Sasha over for dinner twice, but he hadn't warmed up to her yet.

Not only had Amber been away for a couple of months, but I couldn't even remember the last time Alex had stopped by. Had he been by since Amber's mother had instigated her new rules? I didn't think so.

I missed them both terribly, along with the intrinsic energy and motivation that seemed to come along with them.

"I know," I told my cat, sighing back into the couch. "I miss them, too, Hunchie."

At the nickname, Hunch opened one judgmental eye. We didn't have the warm kind of relationship that warranted cutsie nicknames, and the look was all it took to put me in my place.

I turned on the TV and skimmed through all of the suggested programs, but I'd already seen every single one of them. *You know you watch too much TV when . . .*

I kept scrolling through different categories and genres and finally came to the only category I had yet to click on: horror.

I'd never been much of a fan of the genre, but I decided tonight, after dreaming about our new business and actually making steps to put it in motion, I was in the mood for something fresh. Besides, many of the "horror" movies didn't look gory as much as suspenseful. I settled on a new one starring Blake Lively.

Two hours later, despite Hunch's protests, I had him snuggled tight in my arms. I didn't think I'd taken a breath in at least thirty minutes.

"I'm sorry," I told my cat, finally letting him go. He shook out his fur in a typical doglike fashion and hopped off the couch and out of reach.

But then he looked back at me, and I thought I could see in his eyes that, despite his resolve, he needed the companionship as much as I did.

The next morning, I got out of bed still feeding off my drive to try new things from the day before. Whether it had been stepping into Mayhew Bank after such a long time of avoiding it or ordering signage for the food truck, something had given me an energy I hadn't felt in months. But there was one other agenda item I'd been putting off. I picked up my phone, navigated to the number Amber had given me for her therapist months ago, and dialed.

It turned out Dr. Harrison had a last-minute cancellation and could fit me in this afternoon. I accepted the appointment time and jotted down the address in downtown Honeysuckle Grove.

If I was watching scary movies to keep myself busy, I needed more than a mere distraction. It was time to get my life in order.

Dr. Harrison's office was only a stone's throw from the Town Hall. I sat in the small waiting room across from her secretary, trying not to fidget and feeling like every move I made indicated some sort of statement about my mental health.

The secretary seemed to sense this and kept her eyes directed at her computer screen until finally she looked up and said, "Mallory? Dr. Harrison will see you now."

She led me to a room and opened the door to a red-haired woman with her back to us at a desk and two comfy-looking armchairs. The secretary motioned me toward the closest armchair and then shut the door between us.

I crossed my legs, then uncrossed them. Then crossed them the other way.

Finally, Dr. Harrison turned. She was in her forties, wore glasses halfway down her nose, and looked at me over them. I immediately felt scrutinized and had to remind myself that this doctor came highly recommended by Amber, who rarely made recommendations, at least when it came to people.

"Mallory Beck, right?" she asked, looking from the folder in her hands to me.

"That's right," I told her.

"And what brings you in to see me?"

I only realized now that I might have prepared answers for questions like this one. "Um, well, I guess I'm still grieving over my husband's passing?" I asked, as if she would know if this was true.

"I see. You're awfully young to be widowed. Was it from sickness?"

I shook my head. As refreshing as it was to have this woman point out the obvious and painful truths, I had a hard time coming up with any words to respond to them. "A fire. At the bank. Last winter."

Whether or not Dr. Harrison had heard about the bank fire, she didn't show it. Although, a person would have had to have been hiding under a rock not to have heard about the small-town tragedy where three locals had been killed. "No one expects to lose their spouse so early. How long had you been married?"

"Almost five years."

She went on to ask me about my upbringing. I gave her an overview of my absent mom, my narcissistic dad, and my supportive sister. Then she delved deeper into my and Cooper's history, where we had met, and when I'd known I was in love with him, and what was the worst argument we'd ever had.

Strangely enough, I couldn't come up with much in the way of arguments, but I finally described the insecurity I'd had early in our relationship when Cooper's natural charisma often made it feel like he was flirting with other women. I kept expecting to feel something loosen in my chest the more vulnerable I became with my answers, but I still felt tight inside, almost like I was holding my breath.

I explained this feeling to Dr. Harrison.

She tilted her head in response. "Why do you think that is?"

That was what I was asking *her.* Why did she think I'd just bared my soul? But I took in a breath and tried to quell the automatic anger that had overtaken me. "I don't know." She waited for more. "I mean, maybe I just can't get over the unfairness of him being gone?"

She nodded. "And what have you been spending your time with since losing Cooper?"

This felt easier to talk about. I explained my love for cooking, how I'd teamed up with Amber, and how we were slowly starting a catering business. I also talked about how we'd helped Alex solve several local crimes.

"Murders?" she asked when I'd gone into some detail about the investigation at the Town Hall and then about the one at Amber's uncle's mansion.

"That's right," I told her and couldn't help but sing Amber's praises. Even though it was Dr. Haney, Helen Montrose's therapist, who had suggested Amber spend more time with her mom and less time with me, I found myself trying to convince this therapist of how good we were for each other. "Amber's such a bright girl. I think having something important to focus on has helped her with grieving her dad's death. It's helped both of us," I added.

Dr. Harrison nodded and said, "Mmm. Perhaps."

"Besides, the Honeysuckle Grove Police Department is quite understaffed, and they've really been able to use our help. It's been a win-win, really."

Dr. Harrison seemed to be able to detect my insatiable need to have her see my value in this. "On the outside, perhaps that's how it seems," she finally said. I nibbled my lip to hold myself back from arguing, as I feared my words would sound desperate if I opened my mouth. "But I wonder if what was once simply a curious nature in you has been fed by police drama to an unhealthy degree. In addition to the police work feeding your angst, it seems like it might be a way you're trying to prove your worth, both to yourself and to others. What do you think?"

I hated that she asked me. What could I say? If I disagreed with her, she'd likely just nod and ask, "Is that really what you think?" But I also couldn't bring myself to admit that any of the time I'd spent with Amber and Alex in the last year may have been a mistake.

When I didn't say anything, she added, "Remember, Mallory, that police officers and detectives undergo extensive training on how to deal with day-to-day encounters with the darker sides of human nature. You haven't had that kind of training. It's possible it could be taking a toll. It's even possible it's prolonging your healing process over losing Cooper."

I nodded, not in agreement as much as being afraid of what might come next.

"You said you haven't seen Alex in a while and you haven't been helping with investigations lately, but I still sense a strong angst in you, Mallory."

She wasn't wrong. "Alex is busy with cases he can't share. And Amber needs to focus on her relationship with her mom right now."

Dr. Harrison nodded and made a few notes in her file folder. I wished she would just tell me what she was writing. It was probably a diagnosis about how being abandoned by my mother and then raised by a self-serving father had made me into a woman who wasn't terribly healthy for anyone, least of all an impressionable teenager. She could probably sense my attraction to Alex, even though I hadn't stated it outright, and was about to let me down easy about why Alex was probably avoiding me.

Finally, she interrupted my mental rabbit-trailing. "I sense you have a fair amount of trouble trusting your instincts and deciphering when you're operating from a place of turmoil or insecurity and when you're operating from a place of balance." It sounded a little like psycho-babble to me. "I suspect these tendencies truly started to show themselves with the sudden and shocking death of your husband and are only exacerbated by working on murder investigations."

I waited her out to explain how, exactly, this diagnosis might help me heal and move on. I had the sudden urge to tell her about the church ladies I'd been meeting for lunch in the past few months, but I had a feeling my words would only come out defensive, no matter what I said.

"I'd like to give you an exercise to work on before we next meet," she said.

That made me brighten. I liked exercises. I liked the idea of having something I could actually *do* to grow and heal.

"I'd say since Alex is busy on some cases he can't involve you with, it's a good time to take a break from helping with investigations."

That advice agreed with what my sister, Leslie, had been telling me for months. It made me bristle, but at the same time, I *had* been taking a break, what felt like an extended break, really, and yet I still felt general unrest in my life.

"When you find yourself in a place of angst or suspicion or even a lack of trust in your own instincts, I'd like you to sit down and write out all the questions that are bothering you and all the things you know are true. I feel you are developing a distrustful and suspicious nature that is not serving you. Take note of any disparities that raise your intrigue and then list all the reasons that each disparity is part of normal life and not a complicated mystery that needs solving."

Was I creating complicated mysteries in my mind where there weren't any? I'd done that for several months after Cooper died, convinced there'd been foul play involved in his death. It wasn't until I'd helped solve Amber's dad's murder and was able to uncover obvious and irrefutable clues to the murderer that I was able to see Cooper's death as a horrible, unfortunate accident.

I didn't think I stirred up mysteries in my mind anymore, but research had been my specialty when I'd been with Cooper and he'd needed assistance with plotting his novels. The exercise felt a lot like research, and therefore, it felt very much like something I could handle.

# Chapter Three

EVEN THOUGH I BARELY left the house for the next couple of days, I found myself working on my "homework" for Dr. Harrison several times. I made a list when Sasha forgot to call me about the ladies' lunch and I worried something had happened to her. I watched TV and my mind rabbit-trailed to what kind of sneaky motives characters might have—even while I was watching romantic comedies I'd already seen. Maybe Dr. Harrison wasn't far off in suggesting I had developed a distrustful and suspicious nature that wasn't serving me.

Then Alex called and my nature really showed itself.

"Things are still really busy here. Sorry I haven't called."

"Busy with that secret case?" My curiosity was obvious in my voice.

"Yeah, that. And something else Corbett just assigned to me."

This vagueness, of course, really got my curious mind racing. "Oh, yeah? What's that?" I didn't sound cool or casual in the least.

"I'll drop by tomorrow night. It's easier to show you this new . . . surprise obligation in person." Before I could launch into one of the many questions that sentence had sparked, he turned the conversation onto me. "How have you been? What have you been up to lately?"

I searched my mind for anything that wouldn't be stretching the truth. If I told him exactly how many hours I'd spent in front of my television, that wouldn't look great. And while I wanted to tell him about my visit with Dr. Harrison, that seemed more like an in-person type of conversation, so I could see his reaction to everything she had suggested to me. I didn't want her thoughts about my suspicious nature to rub off on him so he felt like he could no longer tell me anything. "I, uh, well, Amber and I came up with a name for the food truck!"

"You and Amber are hanging out again?" he asked, focusing on the wrong part.

"Well, no, not exactly. But we've been emailing, and at first I suggested the idea of making crepes with different fillings. Then Amber came up with the name: Amber and Mallory's Crepe Express."

A pause followed, and then he focused again on the part I hoped he wouldn't. "You know, if having a healthy and honest relationship with her mother is the goal, maybe spending all this time on email together isn't the most proactive plan."

I gritted my teeth to hold in my response. It wasn't as if Amber and I spent hours and hours emailing each other each day. But I guess part of me felt guilty, too, because I'd emailed her half a dozen times since she'd come up with our crêperie title—usually looking for a reason to do it.

"I should probably let you go. If you're so busy." As usual, I couldn't hide anything, least of all when I felt hurt or berated.

"Just hang on," he said. "Before you go . . . Remember when we were talking about your last name and whether you ever planned to change it?"

I did remember. He'd asked me right in the middle of our first dance at a recent wedding. The question had thrown me, and I hadn't had a very composed reaction. "I . . . Yeah. Sure."

Apparently, today wasn't going to be my day for composed reactions either.

"What do you know about the name Beckford?"

I pulled back from the phone, unsure of what to say or how to react. Maybe he thought I was so attached to Cooper's surname that I should take baby steps to change it? But in truth, I didn't want to change it at all.

"I like the name Beck," I told him for the second time.

"Right, right," he said quickly. "But have you ever heard of the name Beckford?"

"I don't know. Maybe in passing. Why?" As I said the words, I started to wonder if I was only rabbit-trailing in my head again. Maybe Alex was only making conversation. What if it was only my fear that I wasn't grieving properly or healing fast enough that was making me so defensive about my last name? I'd have to talk to Dr. Harrison about that when I met with her next week.

"So you don't know anything about the history of the name?" Answering a question with a question was a tactic Alex usually employed during interrogations. But he didn't leave me time to answer. "What do you know about self-publishing? Did Cooper ever try that?"

Now it definitely felt like an interrogation. I shook my head, even though we were on the phone. "He didn't have to. He was treated really well by his publisher, and he liked to just write the books and let his agent and editor take care of the business end of things." As expected, talking about these details brought a heaviness to my chest, but I pushed through, hoping it would get easier the more I did it.

"So Cooper didn't know much about self-publishing, to your knowledge?"

"I remember him talking about how complicated it was, back when we were in college and he had to learn about it in class. He was thankful when he got a literary agent and a publisher before he'd even graduated, so he didn't have to deal with that end of things."

"Do *you* know anything about self-publishing?" Alex asked.

I laughed. "Believe me, I tuned it out even more than Cooper. I never had much of a head for business. Even Amber seems to know more than me about running a business." I realized quickly that I'd inadvertently brought the conversation back to me spending time with Amber. "I mean, back when Cooper was taking the class about publishing options, we did talk about it. I knew about all the requirements of cover art and hiring editors and expectations of quality writing and what a publisher would take care of if you were lucky enough to find one interested in your work."

"What would you say it would cost to self-publish a novel?"

I thought back to conversations I'd had with Cooper on the subject. Surprisingly, it felt easy to go back to these particular memories, perhaps because they were from the years when I didn't know Cooper as well.

Even so, trying to come up with a number was harder than I expected. "Like I said, you'd have to pay for editing and cover art, but as far as I know, uploading it to all the book retailers is free—they just take a percentage when you sell it."

"And what about promotion? Could you spend a lot of money there?"

I shrugged, even though he wouldn't be able to see it. "I'm sure you could. Cooper once had a publicist contact him about working together. I think he wanted to charge Cooper somewhere in the range of ten grand." When Alex didn't say anything, I added, "But he had a publicist at the publisher, so he said no."

"Hmm." Alex was thoughtful for a moment and paper rustled in the background, as though he might be taking notes. I was about to ask if he had thought about self-publishing some kind of a book when he asked, "Do you think these cover and editing costs could have added up to six digits?"

"Six digits?" I asked.

"Over a hundred thousand dollars."

I laughed. "I'm no expert, but I'm pretty sure you could get those services a lot cheaper than that."

"And so if Cooper were to self-publish, he wouldn't have involved his literary agent in that?"

"Well, no. That's the whole point. If you're going to self-publish, it's either because you can't find an agent and publisher who will do a lot of the business work for you or because you want complete control of every aspect. At least that was Cooper's outlook on the whole thing." Even if it was my overcurious nature, I had to ask. "What's this about, Alex? Are you writing a book?"

A long pause followed. So long I wondered if Alex had hung up. But he finally said, "Something like that. I'll tell you more about it later, but for now, I really should go."

After I said goodbye and hung up, I sat down at my kitchen table to write out a list of everything I found intriguing, if not suspicious, about my conversation with Alex.

- He'd called seemingly to chat, but then only asked me a lot of questions.

- He criticized me seeing Amber at every turn.

- He had never shown interest in book writing before, much less self-publishing.

- He brought up the possibility of me changing my name again, even though I'd already explicitly told him I didn't want to, and even tried to push me toward the name Beckford, like it was some kind of compromise.

- And what was this new "surprise obligation" Corbett
  had unloaded on him?

I tried to come up with logical reasons for everything on my list but only came up with Captain Corbett assigning him more nonpriority cases or Alex using his busyness as an excuse because he no longer felt interested in a relationship with me.

I couldn't seem to come up with a single topic that Alex might want to self-publish a book about.

By the time I finished, I felt like Dr. Harrison's homework assignment was backfiring because the more I brainstormed these topics, the more I decided there had to be a lot more under the surface that I wasn't seeing.

# Chapter Four

THANKFULLY, BEFORE MY CURIOUS nature could get the best of me, my doorbell rang. I rushed over, knowing it wouldn't be Alex, and so by default, I hoped it might be Amber.

I swung open my door, and my smile widened when I saw it was neither.

"Pete! Hi!" I didn't think I'd ever been quite so exuberant when greeting Cooper's old college roommate, certainly not in the past year and a half since Cooper had died. Maybe there was some underlying success to this list making Dr. Harrison had me focusing on after all. "Come in! I didn't know you were in town."

Pete rarely called before he dropped by. Ever since I first met him, he'd been like that—showing up and surprising both of us at a local film festival he knew we were attending or at one of my bake-offs in the culinary arts building.

"Just passing through and thought I'd see if you were around." It was what he always said. I suspected he mostly wanted to check on me and see how I was doing every once in a while, but he wasn't terribly great at doing it nonchalantly.

"You know me. I'm always around," I told him.

He started to take off his shoes—a tradition Cooper had started in our first house. "What's that big beast of a truck doing in your driveway?"

Before he could get his shoes off, I grabbed his arm, slipped my feet into some slides, and said, "Come and see!"

My excitement wasn't as contagious as I hoped. Pete looked around the small interior of my new food truck with a furrowed brow, as if trying to find something wrong with it. "Have you had it checked by a mechanic?"

I nodded, even though I hadn't. But I trusted the farmer who had sold it to me, as his rental kitchen had been fully renovated and he no longer needed it. "Have you eaten?" I pulled some flour and sugar from the miniature pantry that held my dry ingredients and didn't wait for his answer. "Let me show you what I plan to make."

Pete was nothing if not a spontaneous person, but he never seemed to care for spontaneity in me. I suspected this was his way of grieving. He had been so shocked by Cooper's death, as I had, and he couldn't change his own personality, but he could try and prevent tragic surprises from others in his life.

Still, I didn't think he had anything to worry about with the food truck. The farmer had charged me about half of what it was worth.

Twenty minutes later, I had a stack of delicate crepes warming in the food truck oven. It was almost dinnertime, so I kept the flattop grill on to fry up some onion and garlic.

"What can I do to help?" Pete asked.

I was never one to turn down help in the kitchen. Teaching Amber to cook had shown me how therapeutic creating a yummy dish could be. "Do you want to chop this onion for me?"

I held out the knife and the onion, ready to show him how to do it, but he helped himself to both, skinned the onion, and chopped it into surprisingly even dices. He was fast, too.

"Have you done this before?" I asked.

"Only for myself at home, but a bachelor has to make himself attractive to the ladies somehow." He winked.

In truth, Pete had a lot going for him. He was good-looking, had a well-paying steady job, could fix almost anything, and now, apparently, he could cook, too. Cooper and I had tried on many occasions to find him a good woman he could settle down with, but in the end, he was always too picky.

Once the onion and garlic had softened, I added some crabmeat and sharp cheddar and wrapped a dollop of each into a crepe.

There was no room to actually enjoy the crepes in the food truck, so once assembled, Pete followed me back into the house and to my kitchen table.

"This is delicious!" he said after practically inhaling three bites in a row of cheesy goodness. "But, Mallory, I'm not keeping you from anything, right?"

He always asked this, and yet he never called ahead. It felt almost like a test when he asked, as though he was gauging to see how much I'd been able to move on after Cooper. While Amber and Alex and even Sasha always seemed proud of me when I got out of the house and actually did something on my own, with Pete it sort of felt the opposite. Perhaps he was still struggling to move on after Cooper's death, too, and misery did love company.

"No, actually, I was just trying to figure out what to do with myself tonight," I told him honestly. I'd spent several hours on food truck planning and therapy homework today. I was more than ready for some company and didn't want him to get the impression I was too busy for him and leave. "You should stay for a movie or something."

He raised an eyebrow. "No houseguests tonight?"

The last time he'd stopped by was at Christmas, when Alex and Amber were both here. I'd been a little rude, as I hadn't wanted Pete to interrupt our planned celebration, but I had later felt horrible and had made him a huge brunch the next day to try and make up for it. I'd called him a couple of times since then, trying to make sure he hadn't been offended, and he didn't seem so, but tonight, having him stop by, finally put my mind to rest about it.

"No houseguests but you," I told him.

He took another bite, chewed, and then said, "I'd rather not drive back until the morning. Okay if I crash here?" He looked up toward my guest room.

"Sure, of course," I told him. Shortly after Cooper passed, Pete had stopped by more often, and it was never a question. He always stayed. I felt bad that Alex and Amber being here last time made him feel the need to ask.

He nodded and finished his second crepe in two bites. "Okay, great. But before a movie, let me take you out for dessert."

I had a few crepes put aside that I'd planned to fill with whipped cream and berries, but I sensed he really wanted to do something for me.

If only I could make him understand how much his company meant. With Amber grounded from visiting and Alex flip-flopping between evasiveness and accusations, spending time with someone as undemanding and uncomplicated as Pete felt like a breath of fresh air.

"I saw a new frozen yogurt place on my way into town. Have you tried it yet?"

Kim's FroYo wasn't exactly off the highway. In fact, it was right in the downtown core, but in truth, I had been eager to drop by and try a scoop. I'd always loved frozen yogurt, and it was one of those food items I didn't make myself.

"You bet. Let's do it," I told Pete.

Half an hour later, we stood in a long lineup of patrons also waiting to try Kim's new frozen yogurt specialties. I recognized a few people, including Donna Mayberry and one of the other lunch ladies, Shelly, a few places in line ahead of us.

I kept my attention on Pete. If Donna came over, she'd no doubt natter on about local gossip, which would immediately leave Pete out of the loop. I felt her watching us, though, and I wondered what kind of gossip she'd stir up about us by the next day. Thankfully, she didn't leave the line to come and say hello, and I kept Pete busy by asking about his dad's construction business and what kind of work he'd been busy with lately. He kept lobbing regular questions about my food truck plans back at me.

Again, I found Pete refreshing. While Alex had come across as judgmental because I'd emailed Amber a few times, Pete genuinely cared about what I was interested in, and I didn't have to watch my words with him, no matter how much I talked about my plans for the food truck.

"I saw Tanner and the kids at Easter," he said, changing the subject and surprising me. Tanner was Cooper's older brother.

"Oh, yeah? Where'd you run into them?" A wave of shame came over me. I hadn't seen Tanner since Cooper's funeral. I'd spoken to their parents a couple of times, but I'd been having so much trouble with my own grief, I couldn't bear being in a room with others and imagining over and over again what it would be like to lose a son or a sibling. How would I feel if something happened to Leslie?

Pete shrugged, looking bashful about it. I ducked to keep eye contact and force an answer. Finally, he came up with, "Well, Dennis and Rita . . . they weren't going to do the Easter thing this year."

Understandable. Dennis and Rita—the Beck parents—had made a pretty big deal about Easter ever since Cooper and Tanner were kids. Apparently, they'd hidden Easter eggs right up until their grown kids were adults and only stopped when

Tanner had kids so they could keep the tradition going with their grandkids.

"So you went over to visit the kids?" I asked.

Pete shrugged with one shoulder. "I don't know. I felt like we all needed a bit of lightness back in our lives. I told Rita I'd take care of everything, but that we'd all be over on Easter Sunday."

"So you did the whole Easter egg hunt for the kids yourself? And the dinner?" I had to admit, I felt a little left out. But then that feeling was quickly overshadowed by guilt. I rarely checked in on Dennis and Rita, and it sounded like they needed someone to pull them out of their grief at least as much as I had.

"Yeah, the plastic eggs full of candy, the turkey. You know, the whole nine yards, as Rita would say." His face reddened. I had so much admiration for Pete—not only checking in on me, despite the long drive to do it, but checking up on Cooper's whole family.

"Wow, that's really awesome that you would do that," I told Pete. "Next time you plan anything for them, I'd be happy to help."

He smiled, and his embarrassment seemed to fade just as we made it to the front of the line. Pete turned to me. "Mint chocolate chip, right?"

I was amazed he remembered. But now that I knew he was somewhat of a foodie, I realized I shouldn't be surprised. I remembered his favorite, too. "As long as you order the salted caramel for yourself."

We made it back to my place just after eight. If he hadn't come by, I'd probably be getting ready for bed and turning in early, as I did quite often these days. But I stifled my yawn and led him to the living room, where Hunch sprang up from where he'd been dozing on the couch the second he saw I had company.

He padded to the edge of the room and perched in the doorway to the kitchen.

"Come on, Hunch. It's Pete. You remember Pete."

Pete dropped into my couch and puffed a pillow up behind him, unoffended. "Don't tell me *you're* talking to that cat now, too?"

Pete and I used to make fun of Cooper for the same thing, and I hadn't thought about that in so long it made me laugh. "I suppose I am," I told him.

Pete wasn't much of a cat person. I hadn't been either until recently, when Hunch and I had come to an understanding of sorts about sharing a house and the loss of the person we loved most.

"Of course you are." Pete shook his head. "Now what are we watching?"

After Pete scrolled through my Netflix screen and suggested a dozen movies I had already seen, I admitted reluctantly, "I guess I watch a lot of TV."

He handed me the remote as I settled onto the couch beside him. "Well, then I think it's up to you to pick something you haven't seen."

When I skipped down to the horror and thriller section, his eyes widened. But I knew these were the types of movies Cooper and Pete used to watch together, so I said, "I haven't seen any of these, except that one with Blake Lively. Why don't you choose something that looks good?"

He pointed to one that looked a little gory for my taste, but I navigated over and clicked on it. I didn't really care what we watched if I had company.

As he got it started, I skipped back to the kitchen to make a bag of microwave popcorn. "What would you like to drink?"

"You have any beer?"

I hadn't been buying beer since Cooper had died, but I looked in the back of my pantry, and sure enough, there were still a couple of bottles there. "It's not cold," I called.

"Just throw it in a glass with an ice cube. If you wouldn't mind," he added.

That wasn't the way most beer connoisseurs would take theirs, but I liked that Pete was relaxed about stuff like this. Being an aspiring chef, I could get caught up in the "rules" a little too much.

In fact, it was such a refreshing thought that I popped open two beers, added ice cubes, and brought them back to the living room with the bowl of popcorn.

An hour into the movie, the popcorn was gone—mostly from me incessantly eating it to calm my nerves, and I'd even drained my beer. So much for not being much of a beer drinker. Pete still had half a glass and looked perfectly relaxed. I was glad. I wouldn't want to get up and leave him to go and fill his drink. In the part of the movie we'd just watched, a woman had been walking home alone at night through the darkened streets with the creepiest music as a backdrop. The woman hadn't been a character in the movie until now, so I was bracing for the moment she'd probably get killed off. Thanks to years of plotting murder mysteries with Cooper, I knew how storytelling worked.

"You okay?" Pete asked me for at least the tenth time.

I nodded but didn't answer, for fear my voice would shake. In truth, I had a love/hate relationship with this kind of tension. It was like riding up a steep hill on a roller coaster. It stops you from thinking about anything else, and it's really not harmful in the end, but it sure does a job on a person's nervous system.

The woman walked through a dark doorway, and even though the music escalated, nothing happened. She walked up a shadowy stairway. Still nothing but intense music. In through her apartment door . . .

Nothing. And then the music stopped.

It wasn't until she walked into her bathroom and I saw the shadow behind the door that my heart went berserk. I couldn't watch and turned to bury my face in Pete's shoulder. He put a hand on my hair to help shield my eyes, and when the woman's shrill scream rang out, I cringed into him farther.

Only seconds later, a calm and lighthearted piano line grew in the background to let me know we were on to the next scene. I started to pull away, to turn and figure out what I'd missed and how it tied into the greater story, but Pete's hand still rested heavy on my hair.

His face was so close, and before I knew what was happening, he leaned in to kiss me.

"What? No!" I jerked away, only realizing a second later that my reaction had been ridiculously abrupt because of the tension still deep in my bones.

Pete sprang up from the couch. "Sorry! Sorry! I thought . . . "

I shook my head. "No, I'm sorry, it's just . . . " I looked up at him, searching for something to say, but his face was turned away, and it seemed we were both completely at a loss for words.

"I should go," he said.

"No, you don't have to." My words held little conviction, as I just wanted this uncomfortable moment to be over. I forced a breath. "Really, Pete. It's too far to drive this late at night."

But he was already striding for the front door. "No worries, Mallory. I'm wide awake. Might as well get back so I don't have to call in late for work tomorrow."

His voice was curt. I'd hurt his feelings. I was certain it was only a strange misinterpretation of the moment, as so many different emotions had had me all discombobulated, too.

But I was still in no position to make him feel less awkward until I dealt with my own guilty and awkward feelings.

And so I let him go without a fight.

# Chapter Five

I FINALLY FELL ASLEEP at nearly two in the morning—first trying to calm down over the movie and then worrying about Pete driving all the way back to Pennsylvania so late at night. As soon as I'd calmed down, I phoned him to make sure he was okay and that he realized I, of anyone, understood having mixed-up feelings and doing or saying things I regretted.

But I only got his voice mail, so I had to leave some semblance of that as a message. I asked him to call me back as soon as he got home so I knew he was safe, but by the next morning, I still hadn't heard a word.

Was he that embarrassed? Or had he fallen asleep at the wheel and driven off the road?

I suspected I should make a therapy list about this as Dr. Harrison had suggested, but instead, to distract myself from these questions, I dealt with another item that had been bothering me since last night. I picked up the phone and dialed Cooper's parents' number, which I still knew by heart. Rita picked up on the second ring.

"Hi, Rita. It's Mallory."

A pause followed, and her tone dropped from what had been a somewhat bright hello. "Oh. Mallory. How nice to hear from you." Her words only punctuated what a poor excuse for a daughter-in-law I had been.

"I'm sorry I haven't been in touch. Time seems to slip away on me." It was the only excuse I could come up with, short of telling her I'd done everything in my power over the past year *not* to think about them and everything they'd lost.

"I'm sorry, too, dear," she said. And then a long pause followed. If I wasn't so tired from staying up half the night, I probably would have called with something to actually say.

"Pete said he saw you at Easter," I blurted the moment it came to me.

She sighed what sounded like a happy sigh. "Yes, he insisted we do things up right for the grandkids. I have to admit, it lifted my spirits a little as well."

Now I felt extra guilty for not making any effort to make their lives a little easier. "I wish I had known. I'd have been happy to help." My words felt like too little too late, but at least they were something. They opened the door for Dennis or Rita to call if they felt the need. At least that was the hope.

"It was all very last minute, but believe me, it was nice to have something to focus on."

"Have you gotten back to work yet?" Rita used to work at the senior center where Cooper's grandma lived. She'd taken a leave after Cooper's death.

She sighed again, this one not so happy. "I wanted to. And I tried to go in once or twice, but there's just too much talk about death there. I had an interview set up for another job—here at the local hotel. But I had to cancel when another appointment came up."

It sounded like the same kind of excuse I gave about not getting back to a job or not getting the food truck on the road just yet. So I had sympathy, for sure. "What kind of appointment? Is everything okay?" I figured I'd better rule out anything serious.

"A detective came into town, wanting to talk to Dennis and me. Apparently, it couldn't wait."

I pulled back from the phone for a second, wondering if I'd heard her correctly. "A detective? What did the detective want?"

"Oh, he was just asking about Dennis's brother, Ron." She said this plainly, as if I should know what she meant.

"Dennis's brother?" I asked.

"Oh, did Cooper never tell you about his Uncle Ron?"

"I don't think so." I sat up on the couch, wondering how a detective might be involved in Cooper's uncle's life. Did this make me overly suspicious? I wasn't sure.

Rita sighed one more time. "Ron's been in and out of prison for all the years I've known him. He's been involved in criminal activity in Pennsylvania, everything from stealing from local stores to orchestrating illegal moneymaking schemes. He even knifed a corner store clerk a few years back. He doesn't care who he hurts in the process, and he has a whole group of underhanded accomplices, almost like a middle-aged gang. Dennis and I even changed our last name shortly after Tanner was born to distance ourselves from the man. It just felt too dangerous when people from Ron's crew would mistakenly turn up on our doorstep looking for him."

Wow, I was surprised Cooper had never shared this with me. Then again, when we weren't plotting mystery novels, Cooper tended to want to protect me from the harsh realities of the world.

Before I could comment, she went on. "Having young kids just made us not want to be associated with Ron Beckford, and even hearing the name again from the detective made me shudder in fear. I hear he's out of prison again now. At least that's what the detective told me."

"Beckford?" I asked, stunned. That was the name Alex had asked me about, I was sure of it.

"Yes. He'd fallen off our radar, but Ron Beckford is still a pretty big name in Pennsylvania underground crime, apparently."

"And who was this detective that wanted to question you?" I had to ask.

Ruffling papers sounded in the background, and I could picture Rita shuffling things around her always-messy dining room table, looking for a business card. "It was a Detective Martinez."

I sat with my mouth open, unable to coax any kind of reply. It didn't matter. Rita had more to say.

"Hmm. It says he's from Honeysuckle Grove, West Virginia. It's so strange that he's from your hometown."

Strange indeed. Was this the secret case Alex had been working on? If it had to do with Cooper's family, I supposed it made sense why he couldn't tell me, but I was freaked out. Why would a detective from Honeysuckle Grove be assigned to a case involving crime in Pennsylvania?

Ron Beckford was recently out of prison. Would he have some reason to look *me* up? Was that why Alex asked if I'd heard the name?

The second I got off the phone with Rita, I made a long therapy list to try and explain away my questions, but the list only stirred up my anxiety more.

None of this made sense. I had to figure out a way to get Alex to tell me what was going on.

# Chapter Six

ALL DAY, I COULDN'T stop thinking about why the Ron Beckford case would have landed in Honeysuckle Grove and on Steve and Alex's caseload. It had to have something to do with me or Cooper, then. Didn't it? Or was I only being paranoid? Alex had suggested he'd come by for dinner tonight, and so as I cooked, I thought of different ways I could pry, without getting him into trouble.

Then again, he'd said he was bringing over a surprise new obligation. Maybe he planned to talk to me about this case in person. The best-case scenario would definitely be if he told me whatever this had to do with Cooper's family, without me having to pry for clues.

I'd left my therapy list alone since this morning, as it only seemed to stir up more unanswerable questions within me. Still, I couldn't get my mind off my swirling thoughts and ended up cooking the whole day to try and release my anxiety.

I started out by preparing a roast to slow cook for the day, but after I browned the onions and carrots, seared the roast on all sides, and added the seasoned meat to my slow cooker, I realized I wouldn't simply be able to sit around and wait for it to cook.

I hadn't made Yorkshire pudding since culinary school, but today was the day to resurrect that recipe. The baked savory pudding with meat juices would make a much better accompaniment than plain old buns. While searching through my potato recipes, I came across a wild mushroom soup with bacon that I couldn't get out of my head. So I made that, too, along with a chocolate soufflé and some berry and whipped cream crepes for dessert.

By the time my doorbell rang just after six, my kitchen looked like a well-stocked buffet. I hoped Alex was hungry.

"Come on in," I called, pulling my Yorkshire pudding from the oven. I had timed it perfectly, so it would still be warm and billowy by the time we sat to eat.

When the doorbell rang again, I stopped what I was doing and looked toward the kitchen doorway. That was strange. Alex didn't usually bother with the bell. Had I forgotten to unlock my front door?

I wiped my hands and strode for my entry, surprised to see Hunch there, staring at the door with his back arched high. His fur pricked out in all directions.

"What is it, Hunch?" I barely had the question out when a high-pitched yelp sounded from the other side of the door. I furrowed my brow and opened the door, but the second I did, two things happened at once.

Hunch let out a cacophony of hisses and yowls that made it sound as though he was being tortured by fire. And a medium-sized German shepherd puppy barked and leaped toward my open door, despite the short leash Alex held him with tight at his side a second ago.

As a knee-jerk reaction, I shut the door before the dog could get to me or, worse, Hunch. The dog jumped at my front door, and Alex called, "No! Bad dog! Down, Hunter," on the other side.

A few seconds later, the noise on the other side of my door quieted. Alex seemed to have the dog under control, but I was still not about to open my door again with Hunch sitting out in the open like the dog's next meal. Sure, my cat was fearless when it came to death-defying situations, and he would even go up against a full-grown tiger, but dogs of any size were his one kryptonite.

I looked around my entryway, trying to figure out how to get outside to Alex—or to get him in. Hunch still had his back arched, on alert, not taking his eyes from my front door.

I had a decorative chair in the corner that I sometimes used to put on or take off my boots. I slid it toward my front closet and tapped the upper shelf. "Come here, Hunch. Why don't you sit up here for a minute?"

He glanced over at me for the briefest second, then turned back and kept his eyes trained on my front door.

I sighed. My cat didn't like being told what to do, but I wasn't about to let him hold me prisoner inside my own house either. "Well, suit yourself. But I'm going outside to see Alex."

I reached for the door handle, and Hunch took off like a dart past me and barely touched the chair as he launched himself up to the shelf in my closet. I pulled the chair away, as Hunch would have no trouble jumping down from that height if he decided he wanted to, but hopefully, the dog wouldn't be able to reach him.

Then I went back for the door and slipped through an opening barely big enough for me before closing it again.

I found Alex squatted and talking quietly to the dog, who immediately spotted me and tried to leap away from Alex again. This time, Alex had a better hold on the leash.

"Hunter?" I asked with a raised eyebrow as he stood again, keeping the dog tight at his side. The dog didn't seem like the serious or threatening personality to wear that name.

Alex let out a heft of a breath, as if even the explanation of this dog was exhausting. "Apparently, Corbett knows a breeder that deals in police dogs. He got a good deal on him and assigned him to me and Bradley to work with. Except he's barely six months old, so not actually old enough to work."

"So you've basically just inherited a puppy?" I asked. The dog was cute, but as if it wasn't bad enough that Alex's captain often had his priorities mixed up when it came to the importance of cases, this would make it practically impossible for Alex to get any work done.

"I wish it were that easy." Now that Hunter had calmed down some, Alex kept a tight rein on him with one hand while stroking the fur under one of his ears with the other. This seemed to calm the dog even more. "I'm driving into Morgantown three times a week, as that's the closest police dog training unit. They're all telling me Hunter is too young to start his training, but Corbett is overeager to have a dog on the force, so he's been insisting."

I shook my head. "Like you don't have enough to do." I looked down at the dog's big brown eyes and quickly realized none of this was the puppy's fault. I squatted to say hello, and when I did, Hunter placed a big lick of a kiss across my cheek.

Even though Alex said, "No, Hunter," it made me giggle.

After scratching him behind the ears as Alex had, and giving him a little love, I stood again. "I have a huge amount of food inside . . . " I glanced over my shoulder at my front door. "But, well, I don't think it's the best idea to have Hunch and Hunter together in my house."

Even as I said the words, I could envision a chase throughout both floors that would result in everything I owned and loved being torn to shreds.

"I *know* that's not a good idea," Alex said with a smirk. "Sorry I didn't consider Hunch sooner." He sighed. "The truth is, I really shouldn't stop for dinner, anyway. I just thought I should introduce you to Hunter in person." He took a step away. Hunter was surprisingly obedient and took a step with him.

But suddenly, I remembered my purpose for all my cooking in the first place. I had to find a way to ask about Ron Beckford. "But isn't Hunter keeping you away from your work, anyway?"

He nodded. "Mickey's taking a couple of shifts with him a week. Like tomorrow, I have to take a run into Pennsylvania, so I'll drop him at Mickey's on my way."

Mickey Bradley was Alex's mostly incompetent partner on the force, but I was glad to hear he could at least handle dog sitting. Alex took another step away, the suggestion of all the work he had to do making him eager to get back to it.

"I have to at least get you a to-go container," I said quickly. "Slow-roasted beef and all the fixings." When his eyes lit up, I decided I didn't have to list off all the sides I'd prepared. "I'll just be two minutes."

When I returned inside, Hunch still loomed above from the closet, staring at the door with wide eyes.

It took me about four minutes, in actuality, to pack up the food, but I was sure Alex wouldn't leave with the suggestion of roast beef on the table, so to speak. As I packed his food, I thought about what purpose he might have for traveling to Pennsylvania. It had to have something to do with the Ron Beckford case. And if his partner, Mickey, was staying behind, did that mean Alex was going alone?

I didn't like that, but more so, I didn't like that Alex was about to leave without giving me any answers. I'd had myself convinced that he would come over tonight to tell me all about his case and how it related to Cooper's family.

When I returned outside with a giant food container, I said, "Hey, where in Pennsylvania are you headed?"

"A small town just outside Lancaster." He was distracted. With the opening of my door, Hunter had leaped and yanked at his leash again.

Cooper's brother, Tanner, lived in Lancaster. As the thought occurred to me, I spoke it. "Any chance I could catch a ride with you? I have an old friend in Lancaster I've been meaning to catch up with."

Alex pulled Hunter toward his car. "Uh, sure. Yeah, I guess."

I followed him toward his car and placed his food container on his passenger seat while Alex secured Hunter in his carrier in the backseat. "Okay, great!" I said, probably too enthusiastically. "Pick me up in the morning. I'll be ready!"

# Chapter Seven

THANKFULLY, TANNER BECK, COOPER'S older brother, was off work the next day. I would have pretended I had a reason to spend the morning in Lancaster, regardless, but it was nice not to have to lie to Alex.

I had texted Tanner to ask him if he had any time if I dropped into town, as I was afraid if I heard his voice, I might back out on actually seeing him in person.

Tanner had always reminded me of Cooper, and that was probably a big part of the reason why I'd remained distant from their family since Cooper's death. But it was time to start working through these hurdles. If I didn't do it on my own, I was certain Dr. Harrison would soon be suggesting it.

Alex picked me up just after nine. He wore his plainclothes police uniform, but they were flecked with dog fur.

"Did you have to deal with Hunter already this morning?" I asked, following him from my front door to his car.

Alex nodded. "He's staying nights at my place for the time being, as we don't have any kind of kennel set up at the station. In good news, he finally slept through the night last night."

Hunter was still a puppy, sure, but shouldn't he have been sleeping through the night long ago? As if Alex could hear my internal question, he answered me as he backed out of my driveway and turned toward the highway.

"He's been quite excitable since relocating to my house. I have a crate for him to sleep in at night, but he's used to being around other dogs, not all on his own, so I've been up with him a lot in the last week so he didn't feel so lonely."

I could tell by the way Alex spoke about his new police dog that he'd already developed somewhat of a bond with him. While it had meant a few sleepless nights, their connection seemed to come a lot quicker than my hard-won bond with Hunch had.

"So what's in Lancaster?" I asked as casually as I could manage.

"Just stopping at the county prison there to talk about a suspect in a case."

"A case?" launched off my tongue before I could hold it back.

Alex looked away from the highway and at me with a serious expression that meant "Don't ask."

And so I nibbled my lip to keep the rest of my many questions in. That lasted for about five minutes. "I was talking to Cooper's parents the other day," I said, figuring at least if he knew how much I was already aware of, it might open the door for him to tell me more. "They live right outside Lancaster."

"Mmm. Is that who you're going to visit?" He kept his voice even. I couldn't tell if he was avoiding the conversation or if it just hadn't occurred to him that I might have heard about him calling them about Ron Beckford.

"No, today I'm stopping in to see Cooper's brother, Tanner. I haven't seen him or his kids in a long time. But, you know, funny thing, when I was talking to Dennis and Rita—"

"Oh, wow. I didn't realize I was so low on gas. Having Hunter around all the time distracts me from a lot of the everyday stuff of life, you know?" He signaled and took the next exit.

I sat there with my mouth agape. He was definitely avoiding the conversation. But why?

I didn't have a chance to find my voice and ask before he pulled up beside a gas pump. This rural station didn't have a pay-at-the-pump option, and so Alex had to go inside the station to pay. While he did, my gaze drifted around the car, looking for the words that were escaping me.

Instead of finding the right words, I saw on the backseat a lot of dog hair and a beige file folder, the contents of which had spread across the backseat with Alex's sharp turn off the highway.

My gaze couldn't seem to help from roaming over the exposed papers. One had a printed line reading "Account number: 428 079."

Underneath that were several names with question marks in Alex's handwriting.

Ron Beckford?

Peter Becker?

Cooper Beck?

Mallory?

I'd never heard the name Peter Becker, but more concerning was seeing *my* name there alongside Ron Beckford's. Not to mention Cooper's.

Did Alex think I had some kind of information about this case he was working on? But if he did, why hadn't he asked me? He knew I'd tell him anything. Didn't he?

As he left the gas station and headed toward the car, I made a split-second decision, pulled out my phone, and held it under my arm to snap a quick photo. It was wrong. I knew that. But if Cooper's family was somehow involved in this case—if *I* was somehow involved—and Alex wouldn't talk to me, what choice did I have? At the very least, I'd spend some time Googling Ron Beckford and Peter Becker to see how those names might align with me and/or Cooper.

When we got back on the road, Alex quickly redirected our conversation to his new dog. He already had a zillion stories about how Hunter had knocked everything off Captain Corbett's desk and the havoc he caused every single time Alex had him off-leash, even for two seconds.

His stories were clearly a diversion, but the more he went on, the more anxious it made me. What kind of mystery was swirling around me without me even being aware of it? Why did Alex feel the need to hide so much from me? By the time we took the second exit to Lancaster, I hadn't said another word to Alex, but I'd worked myself up into an awful sweat.

Tanner Beck's apartment was right in downtown Lancaster. I'd been into town a handful of times since Cooper had died but had not so much as texted Tanner or his wife. Part of me felt guilty that it'd taken being motivated by my own need for information to do it, but the other part of me knew that if this was what it took, it was still probably healthy for me to at least visit.

"You're sure he's home?" Alex asked as he pulled up to the curb I'd directed him to.

The apartment building was only three-stories tall and had flower gardens surrounding it on the three sides I could see. The neighborhood was quiet, and a couple of moms with strollers walked along the sidewalks. If a family couldn't afford a house in town, I supposed this was a good second option.

I nodded. "Yes, he said he'd be around all day."

"Should I pick you up here again when I'm done?"

I nodded again. "Just text me. You don't have to come up." I said this, but I was curious if he'd create a reason to come to the door and ask Tanner any pointed questions. Or maybe he'd done that already, on the same day he'd visited Dennis and Rita.

Two minutes later, I was through a small courtyard and at Tanner's first-floor apartment door. He quickly answered my knock.

"Mallory!" He pulled me into a hug as I tried to catch my breath. While looking similar to Cooper with his bronze skin and curly black hair, Tanner had aged at least five years in the last one. At only thirty-two, his hair had started to gray at the temples. But that realization immediately brought with it the reminder that Cooper would never age.

"It's so good to see you," I said in a choked voice.

He pulled me into his apartment. His eyes looked droopy and sad, but they brightened as I came inside. Maybe it was because of the fog of grief I'd endured alone in my own house, but his thankfulness for me being here was actually palpable.

"Is Laney home?" His apartment was dark, and it was only just after ten in the morning, so I hoped she wasn't still sleeping.

His forehead furrowed. "I . . . I guess you didn't hear?"

I followed him toward his kitchen, noticing a dank smell along the way. When we reached his kitchen, I could immediately tell why. It looked like it hadn't been cleaned in a month. The sink overflowed with dirty dishes, and the counter was littered with crumbs and dirty paper plates.

This was no place to raise young kids.

But the moment the thought occurred to me, Tanner's last question made sense. I turned to him. "Laney and the girls left?" I guessed.

He nodded solemnly and dropped into a kitchen chair. The table was covered in papers and a bowl with dried soup of some kind, but I ignored it and sat across from him.

"My parents didn't mention it to you?"

I shook my head, feeling guilty all over again for staying out of touch. "I just spoke to them for the first time in a long time the other day."

He bowed his head. "I wasn't doing so well after . . . after Coop . . . " His voice choked on his brother's name. "I've been suffering from depression and anxiety. When I stopped going into work, Laney said she couldn't stay and try to help if I didn't want the help." He sank lower and lower into his chair as he spoke, clearly feeling a weight of guilt from this.

"Are you getting help? For the depression?" I asked.

He shrugged one shoulder. "My doctor put me on antidepressants, but I got awful headaches and couldn't sleep so I had to stop taking them."

"Well, are you doing anything else? Are you seeing a counselor or a therapist?"

He tapped a spoon at the dried soup and didn't answer, which I took as a no.

"I've started seeing someone. I'm still going through my own share of fallout from losing Cooper." It surprised me that I could speak about losing my husband in a calmer way than Tanner, who used to be so strong. Now that I thought about it, Tanner used to be a good ten pounds bigger and more muscular than his brother, but now he looked skinny, like he hadn't been eating. "It's really helped me."

Having Amber around had definitely helped me, too. Looking at Tanner was almost like looking in a mirror of where I might be without her.

He nibbled his lip. "I wouldn't know who to go to or where to start."

"I can ask my therapist for a recommendation here in town, if you're interested."

He looked up at me and nodded. Whether he was genuine or not, I didn't care. I would force this on him if I had to.

We talked more about how long Laney had been gone, and when I pressed him, I got the impression there was still hope for their marriage. He just needed to get his own life on track so he wasn't dragging the whole family down with him. I remembered Laney as having a big heart.

"Your wife is still alive, and I know she loves you," I told him. He took the admonishment, nodding seriously back at me. "Let me help you, like someone helped me."

He nodded and didn't look away. I could feel my offer affecting him.

Tanner let me help him in practical ways all morning, first cleaning his kitchen and living room, and putting in a few overdue loads of laundry, and then calling my therapist's office to get a recommendation in Lancaster. I made him an appointment, remembering how hard it had been for me to make the first one for myself.

As we worked, I peppered him with questions about Ron Beckford and Detective Alex Martinez, but he'd never heard of Alex, and he'd barely heard of his uncle. Apparently, his parents hadn't spoken much about his uncle, the career criminal.

"I think Cooper met him once," Tanner told me as I followed him outside to dump a load of garbage into the bin. As we got comfortable with each other, talking about Cooper had also become more comfortable. I had explained to Tanner how talking with Amber had really helped me heal, and already, he seemed to be taking this to heart.

"Cooper met Ron Beckford?" I confirmed.

He nodded. "I can't remember much of the details, but Coop said this uncle of ours contacted him about some moneymaking scheme. He had no interest and declined, but when he told our parents he'd been talking to Ron, they freaked out and told him to steer clear of that man if that was the last thing he did."

I furrowed my brow. "How long ago was this?"

I figured it must have been long before Cooper and I had met, but Tanner shrugged and said, "I think it was right around the time you two moved to West Virginia."

Strange that Cooper had never mentioned this conversation to me. Then again, during the time we were moving, he'd been on a book deadline and quite scatterbrained with all he had to keep on top of, and I'd been working long hours, trying to prove myself at a new sous-chef position. I supposed it could have easily slipped his mind, especially if he had no interest in his uncle and his schemes.

"Anyway, last I heard, Uncle Ron went to prison again, so probably better that Coop never did get involved with whatever he'd suggested."

Rita had mentioned that Ron Beckford had recently been released from prison, but I figured if Tanner was already suffering from anxiety and depression, he didn't need to worry about this uncle he barely knew of.

"Have you ever heard the name Peter Becker?" I asked.

Tanner shook his head. "Don't think so. The only Pete I know is Cooper's buddy." He smiled and nodded. "Great guy, that Pete."

"I hear he planned a big Easter get-together for the family," I said.

"Yeah, he's been great about dropping in on Mom and Dad. And me, too. I think he planned it mostly so I could see my girls. Well, that and to cheer up Mom and Dad."

Another wave of guilt came over me. "I wish I'd been there to help or thought of doing something like the Easter celebration. I've barely picked up the phone to call you or your parents. It doesn't make me a great daughter-in-law, does it?"

It felt good to say the thoughts that had been plaguing me out loud.

But Tanner raised an eyebrow in response. "*We* haven't been a great family to *you*, Mallory. Did you ever think of that? I mean, you lost your husband and we've been so caught up in our grief, we haven't picked up the phone either."

I shook my head. "But Pete—"

"Pete has a bigger heart than any of us deserve." He laughed, and it was good to hear him laugh again. "You know, we should see if he's free for lunch. Meet him in town?" He looked at me in question.

I needed to get things back to normal with Pete, so I jumped on the idea. "That would be great!"

Tanner called him, and I figured when he got Pete's voice mail, he'd leave a message and leave it at that. But instead, he picked up his phone again right away. I liked seeing Tanner excited, or at the very least, interested in something. "I'll call his dad at the construction site. He can probably tell me when Pete takes his lunch."

I listened to Tanner's side of the conversation while he spoke to Pete's dad. I'd only met Mr. Kline once, but I'd heard plenty about the Greek immigrant who had a rock-hard work ethic and expected nothing less from his son. Pete's dad had forced him to drop out of college when he was a year away from getting his master's degree in creative writing to work at a "real job" with his construction team.

"Oh. When will he be back?" Tanner said, and then after a second, "What's that?"

I could hear rumblings of Pete's dad's disgruntled voice all the way from where I sat across the table. Soon after Tanner hung up.

"Pete's not around today?" I guessed.

Tanner shook his head, twisting his lips and looking disappointed. "His dad is so hard to understand, but it sounded like Pete's away on some writing retreat. Do you know anything about that?"

I probably should have. I *would* have if Pete and I hadn't had that weird interlude a few days ago. He'd called back once since then, in the middle of the night so he knew I wouldn't pick up, and left a short, to-the-point message, letting me know he'd gotten home safely and not to worry.

I still did worry, but I was happy to hear Pete was writing again.

# Chapter Eight

WHEN ALEX PICKED ME up and immediately rambled on about the balmy spring weather, it quickly became obvious he was simply trying to avoid talking to me about his recent appointment.

"How did it go with Cooper's brother?" he asked, switching subjects so fast he sounded like he'd had too much caffeine.

"It was good that I came," I told him honestly. "Tanner's wife left him a few months ago, but I don't think it's too late for them. He just needed a reminder of what's important and a nudge to take better care of himself." Now that I'd been honest about my morning, I felt entitled to ask a more on-the-nose question of my own. "How did it go at the prison?"

He nodded. "Fine, fine."

I could feel him ready to turn the subject back on me, so without much forethought, I launched into another quick question. "Did you talk to Ron Beckford? Or was he already released?"

Alex did a double take away from the road. This was the moment of truth. I had admitted I knew something about the case he was working on. Now it was just a matter of whether or not he would trust me with it.

He didn't speak for several long moments, staring at the road in front of him. I watched him carefully, willing him to feel that it was okay to talk to me about it. Finally, he said, "So you do know the name Beckford?"

"Only since yesterday," I explained, still staring at the side of his stoic face as he focused on the road. His jaw tightened and loosened as he waited for more. "Rita, Cooper's mom, she said you'd been in contact with them, asking about Dennis's brother, Ron Beckford."

When Alex still didn't say anything and only gripped the steering wheel tighter, I had to push. "Alex, what does this have to do with Cooper's family?"

"It's just a money-laundering scheme we're trying to figure out." He shook his head. "I shouldn't have even told you that much."

"Are Dennis and Rita in danger? Why on earth has this landed on your desk in Honeysuckle Grove?"

He snapped a look at me. "Maybe they *are* the danger, Mallory. Did you ever think of that? Perhaps I have to investigate this because all signs are leading to a suspect right in our hometown." He sounded angry.

I pulled back as my mind raced through the list of names I'd seen in his papers on the drive into Lancaster. "Me? Did I do something here? Are you investigating *me?* Why am I listed in your paperwork, Alex?"

Alex spun almost fully around to check the backseat, where his file folder lay intact. "What were you doing looking through my documents?" He gritted the question through his teeth. I was ready for him to tell me how much trouble he could get into for a breach of privacy he'd already been warned about, but instead, he said, "Do you even realize how this will make you look?"

"Make me look?" I was almost shouting now. Really, Alex should pull over for this conversation, but he only sped up, seemingly eager to get me home and out of his car. "But I haven't done anything!"

Had I? I searched my brain. What could I have done that Alex might be investigating?

"I can't have you meddling in this case, Mallory. I have to tell Steve that you were privy to my file—"

I cut him off. "One page! Your file was spread across the backseat, and I couldn't help but see one page with mine and Cooper's and Ron Beckford's names on it. I have no idea what it means, so if you need to tell Steve something, at least tell him the whole truth." I slouched back into my seat and crossed my arms.

He took another deep breath in through his nose, let it out, and sounded a little calmer when he spoke again. "Look, I can't talk to you about this, okay? Steve is going to need to ask you some questions. I'm sure about that now, but if you keep asking me about the case, I won't be able to talk to you at all."

So there it was. The ultimatum.

I was being investigated in relation to Cooper's uncle without knowing why. Alex had been hiding this from me for months. He'd just yelled at me for meddling, and my in-laws might be in trouble.

On top of everything else, I had just come from an emotionally draining time with Tanner. I didn't want to lose Alex or put him in an impossible position, but I also felt about to explode with all of my questions, not to mention angry I was at how Alex kept shutting me down.

Somehow, I either had to try and put out of my mind that I was being investigated for *something*, force a smile onto my face, and pretend everything was normal, or keep pressing him until he told me everything he knew and probably lose one of my best friends in the process.

There wasn't a therapy list long enough for my problems.

# Chapter Nine

I PACED MY KITCHEN floor with Hunch hot on my heels for half an hour before I came up with one useful idea. I couldn't involve Amber in any kind of investigative work, especially one that concerned me, and I wasn't ready to throw away my friendship with Alex to get some answers. I had to trust he knew me well enough that I hadn't been involved in any criminal activity linked to Ron Beckford, at least not with my knowledge. If anything, I was pretty sure he was trying to prove me innocent.

I just wish I knew of what.

And it still left me with no one to talk to. Perhaps it wasn't healthy that I only had two friends close enough to confide my troubles to. I suddenly wished I'd stayed in touch with more of my college friends. Or if only my sister, Leslie, had been willing to listen about my need to put my mind to something useful, even if it was murder investigations, then perhaps I could talk to her about this. If Cooper was still here, he would help me calm down and see the situation from a reasonable perspective, I was sure of it.

My cat let out little *mreowrs* as he followed me across the kitchen. He clearly knew there was another investigation in the works, but talking to him wouldn't be enough. I picked up my phone and dialed Pete. Even though I'd pushed him away, he had come back into my life at the time when I most needed him, and he had to be able to see that.

Maybe calling him would even bring things between us back to normal.

Besides, he knew the Beck family better than I did. He'd known Cooper. He would know if Cooper had had any kind of dealings with Ron Beckford.

Pete's phone went straight to voice mail, which didn't surprise me, but today, instead of leaving another apology, I launched into my questions. "Look, Pete, I don't have anyone else to talk to. Have you ever heard the name Ron Beckford, Dennis's brother? Did you ever hear Cooper talk about him? I think I'm being investigated for something to do with this Uncle Ron or something to do with Cooper, I'm not sure, but whatever it is, I need help to prove I wasn't involved with anything illegal. Can you call me back when you have a chance? I could really use a friend."

While I waited to see if he'd call me back, I switched apps on my phone to my photos. I wanted to look at the paper from Alex's file one more time, but then I had to do the right thing and delete it. What would Alex think if he found out I'd taken a picture of his document? And when Detective Steve Reinhart showed up in all of his official business to question me, at least I could be honest and say I hadn't kept anything from Alex's case file.

I zoomed in one more time to look at my name, scrawled out in Alex's handwriting. I considered how much it must have pained him to write it. All the other names were written in a black pen, while mine was in blue, which made me think he'd been putting off adding me to the list and he'd done it at a later time.

And who was Peter Becker? Was that some sort of derivative of the Beckford name as well? What made Alex think Cooper and Ron were involved in some kind of illegal activity together? Did he have proof? He couldn't. Cooper had been one of the most upstanding people I'd ever known. While all of his classmates made up excuses when their school assignments were late, Cooper would stride right up to his professors and explain he'd made a bad judgment call over the weekend and had spent too much time with his girlfriend, rather than writing.

What evidence could Alex possibly have on Cooper, or on Dennis and Rita, for that matter? Was Alex only jumping to conclusions and looking for something that wasn't there because he felt some envious feelings toward my magnanimous late husband? Cooper had had faults. It just felt more generous not to focus on them now that he was gone.

Which led me to the other possibility. Had there been a darker side to Cooper I simply wasn't letting myself look at? Was he really the man I thought he was? Could there have been a nefarious reason he'd never told me about his Uncle Ron, other than forgetfulness? Could I even trust my own memories of him?

No, if Cooper Beck had been involved in some kind of criminal activity, it was more than likely an accident, something he had been completely unaware of.

Which begged the question, could Cooper have really been involved in something illegal without both of us knowing?

This seemed like the only explanation of why the police thought I was involved. Maybe Cooper hadn't even known he was doing something wrong. That seemed more like my husband than anything. He was a creative genius, sure, but when it came to navigating everyday life or even taking social cues, he often lacked common sense.

One time, when we'd first been looking for a rental house in our college town, we visited five different places we liked and hadn't heard back before I pressed into the conversation and realized Cooper hadn't bothered to check the voicemails on his phone in more than a week.

After that, I'd given my phone number, and we'd had a place secured by the next day.

I kept trying to make myself hit the delete button on the photo of the suspect list that contained my name, but I just couldn't seem to do it. Hunch rubbed back and forth along my shins, seemingly just as interested. There was also that account number at the top. I had no idea how to look into an account number. Should I go to all the banks from here to Lancaster and ask about it?

Before I came up with any other solutions, I noticed another paper behind the one with my name, angled so I could only make out the header.

HONEYSUCKLE GROVE TITLE DEEDS OFFICE.

It reminded me that I never had looked into the other property that was listed in Cooper's name in Honeysuckle Grove. There had been no mention of the property while navigating through Cooper's will and all of his assets. Cooper's literary agent had suggested it was probably just a clerical error, but seeing the name of the title deeds office in black and white, I wasn't sure I believed that.

What if Cooper was somehow involved in illegally buying property with his Uncle Ron? This, at least, was one area I could investigate without crossing any lines with Alex because I had planned to visit the title deeds office long before I'd seen the information in his file.

The only difference was I now had zero faith that it might come out as a clerical error. Something here was wrong.

I was about to find out what.

# Chapter Ten

THE HONEYSUCKLE GROVE TITLE Deeds Office was in a tiny one-room storefront just off Main Street, situated between Arty's Coffee, which served a great homemade éclair, and Oh Sew Simple, a sewing and alterations store.

A bell jangled over the door as I entered, and a young guy of no more than twenty looked up from behind a messy desk that took up the bulk of the small office. He wore a Hawaiian shirt, and his shaggy dark hair brushed his shoulders. The name tag on his chest read: JOSH.

I looked back at the decal on the glass door. I definitely had the right place. Still, I couldn't help but ask, "Is this the title deeds office?"

Josh stood from behind his desk, his eyes remaining on some papers in front of him for a few seconds before looking up. "Sure is. What can I help you with?"

"I'm looking for some information about the ownership of a property here in Honeysuckle Grove. Can you help with that?" I had decided in advance that I wouldn't call myself a special consultant from the police department today, not after the argument Alex and I had just had. Besides, I certainly didn't want to shed more guilt on myself for any kind of crime I may have been involved in, yet knew nothing about.

"Should be able to. What's the address?" Josh sat back down and rustled his mouse to bring a computer screen to life.

"Well, actually, I don't have the exact address. But can you check under a name?" When he agreed, I gave him Cooper's name.

Only a second later, he told me, "I see one property here, but that ownership was transferred to a Mrs. Mallory Beck last year."

He rattled off the address that I was well familiar with. "Yes, that's me. That's my home that I shared with my late husband. But I'm looking for another property. I saw mention of it on the comptroller website for West Virginia. It didn't list an exact address, just a quarter-acre plot in town here."

Josh typed some more, and after flipping through a few screens, he came back with something. "Okay, I see it here. It's over on Marsh Avenue. 2388 is the address. That's also your late husband's?"

I still had no idea. "If this was my husband's property, why wouldn't it have been part of his estate?"

Josh shrugged. I shouldn't have expected him to know anything about wills and estates at his age. I certainly wouldn't have known anything if it hadn't been for Cooper's early passing.

But then Josh studied his screen and tilted his head. "Actually, it says LLC."

"What's that?" I asked.

"It's under the name Cooper Beck LLC, which seems like a company name, more than an actual person." He looked up at me. "Know anything about that?"

I pulled back. I'd never heard of Cooper forming a company. Didn't LLC suggest a corporation? He'd never have been able to figure that out on his own. Maybe I'd have to phone his agent, Mitch Reynolds, again to check in and see if he had set that up for Cooper at some point.

But why wouldn't Cooper have told me, especially if he held another plot of land? The whole idea of it gave me shivers. Maybe Cooper *had* been involved in something illegal, or at the very least something shady, if he'd been keeping big secrets like this one.

I made a note in my notepad to get in touch with Mitch later, as if I might forget. "What about Ron Beckford? Do you have any properties listed in town under his name?" I'd have to look his name up on the comptroller site later. "Or anything under Peter Becker?"

Josh spent a long time searching computer screen after computer screen. During that time, my mind raced through possibilities, and I was glad I didn't have a full-size pad of paper handy or I'd surely be making an extra-long list for Dr. Harrison that included all the wild possibilities I'd already come up with, plus a few new ones.

Like, was Cooper truly guilty of some kind of a crime?

Had he been keeping secrets from me through our entire marriage?

Could I have unwittingly become his accomplice in something illegal?

Finally, Josh looked up. "Nope. Not a thing here for a Ron Beckford, Ronald Beckford, or Peter Becker. I checked and double-checked."

Even though he was young and a little rough around the edges, the guy seemed diligent enough. "What about the property under Cooper Beck LLC? What can you tell me about it?"

A minute later, Josh was back on that screen. He turned his monitor so I could see the title deed he'd brought up. "The originals are filed away," he told me, motioning to three large metal filed cabinets along the wall behind him. "But here's an electronic copy."

I snapped a photo of his screen with my phone.

"Oh, actually, you're not allowed to photograph official government documents." He sounded nice enough about it, and I didn't want to get the guy in trouble, but I still hoped I'd gotten a good enough shot to see later.

"Sorry about that." I pocketed my phone, for once glad I'd followed Amber's advice in asking for forgiveness, rather than permission. "So if this property is owned by a corporation, how do I find out more about who the owner of this corporation is?"

Josh furrowed his brow, looked down and around his messy desk, and then back up at me. "I don't think I've ever been asked that. I have no idea."

I looked around the small one-room office. "Is there a manager or someone I could ask?"

Josh twisted his lips. "Mrs. Bozeman only works Fridays these days, but she's, like, eight-five, and she hired me when I was straight out of high school because she said she needed someone with a 'young memory,' so I doubt she'd know either."

I sucked in a breath and let it out in a huff.

Another dead end.

At least I had found out that this wasn't a clerical error. Still, I was apt to believe Cooper had somehow been as in the dark about this corporation as I was.

I thanked Josh, said goodbye, and headed home to call Mitch Reynolds and study the one photo I'd gotten without permission.

# Chapter Eleven

WHEN I BLEW UP the photo I'd taken at the title deeds office on my laptop, nothing about it looked familiar. Not the address, not the buyer's LLC address in Strasburg, Pennsylvania—a town not far from where Tanner lived—and not the messy, unrecognizable signature. There could have been an R or a P at the beginning, and a K in the middle, but that didn't help me one bit.

I Googled Cooper Beck LLC and receive a lot of results for Cooper's novels, but nothing that included LLC or looked like any kind of company website.

After that, I returned to the comptroller website. It took a fair amount of navigating to sift through the Ronald and Ron Beckfords listed in Pennsylvania. I made note of all of them, but none of them came up with any results when I cross-referenced them with either the address on Marsh Avenue or the one listed on the photo in the title deed.

Then I made another therapy list.

Maybe Mitch Reynolds set up a company for Cooper but hadn't had time to tell him about it before the accident? But I sent an email to Mr. Reynolds to ask after an LLC company in Cooper's name and heard back from his secretary within the hour that he had no knowledge of any such thing.

Maybe a fan set up a company in Cooper's name? This reminded me of the time that Cooper had a young fan running around, impersonating him. While it freaked me out, it had turned out to be harmless. I added the word HARMLESS to this note on my therapy list, hoping it might make me feel less anxious.

But no matter what the explanation, either Cooper or I were being investigated by the police for *something*, and that didn't seem harmless.

I picked up the phone to see if I could move up my next appointment with Dr. Harrison. I kept telling myself I must be overreacting. It must be my hypersensitive imagination that was throwing me into constant anxiety and suspicion.

If that were the case, I needed Dr. Harrison to at least give me a few viable options for why I might be under a secret investigation that Alex couldn't even tell me about.

When my phone rang, I snatched it up, assuming it would be Dr. Harrison's office calling me back. "Hello? Can she fit me in anytime today?" I said in way of an answer.

A pause followed, then Amber's dubious voice. "Can *who* fit you in for *what*?"

I was so surprised—and happy—to hear from Amber, I immediately told her the truth. "I've been seeing Dr. Harrison. Or, at least, I've seen her once. You were right. She's super helpful."

"Whoa, slow your roll, there, Mallory. If she's helping so much, why do you sound like you just swallowed an auctioneer?" In comparison, Amber's voice was slow and relaxed, and it really did prove how hyped up on coffee I sounded.

The second I thought that, I used it as my excuse. Under no circumstances was I going to involve her in another investigation after her mother had made it clear this was one of the primary reasons she couldn't see me—even if it was to prove my own innocence. "Oh, yeah, I just grabbed a mocha from that coffee shop, Arty's?" I didn't wait for her recognition. At least this much was true. "He must have given me a double-shot."

She laughed under her breath. "Yeah, he does that. Hey, Mom was supposed to pick me up over an hour ago, and Seth's working. Any way I could get a ride."

I opened my mouth, then shut it again. There was a half-decent bus system in Honeysuckle Grove. Sometimes you had to wait for an hour, but I happened to know you could get most places, even Amber's home, via the bus. At the same time, I didn't want to do anything to make this break from Amber longer than it needed to be. "You think your mom forgot?" I hedged. "Did you try calling her?"

Amber huffed out a breath. "She's not picking up, which tells me she's probably overmedicated again."

I waited for her to push me like she used to and add in a snarky tone that if I didn't want to help her out that was fine. But she stayed silent on the other end.

I couldn't help myself. If her mom was dropping the parenting ball again, no matter how much I might understand, I was going to be there to help Amber. "You're at the school?" I asked. When she confirmed this, telling me she'd had to come in for a test, I told her I'd be there in ten. "But straight home," I added before hanging up.

I didn't realize how much I missed Amber until she hopped into my passenger seat and smirked at me like no time had passed at all.

"Can't I at least stop by to see Hunch?" she begged me.

"Maybe next time," I told her, having no idea when that might be. Thankfully, she let it go.

The moment I got onto the road, she started peppering me with questions. "What have you been doing lately? Helping Alex with any investigations?"

I shook my head. "He's too busy with his case with Steve. But I have been getting the food truck in top shape. I even ordered a magnetic sign for it." I had a sudden thought and blurted it before I could rethink it. "Hey, I thought about setting up an LLC for our catering company. You're taking a business class, right?"

She raised an eyebrow. "A corporation for our little Crepe Express? It's probably more work than it's worth. You have to go through the Bureau of Corporations and Charitable Organizations, and it's a huge hassle, from what I hear."

"A huge hassle? Like there's a lot of paperwork to be filed?" That could be good news. The more paperwork I could find, the more likely I might come across a name of someone alive I could ask about it or some reason why a person would have set up a corporation in Cooper's name.

Amber shrugged. "They're usually used by companies that are really worried about protecting themselves or who want to hide some of their dealings. If you're really concerned about going legit, just set up a partnership or sole proprietorship. As long as we have a business license, good insurance, and the right health permits, we shouldn't have to worry about being sued."

That was all I got out of her before we arrived at her house, and I was determined to get her out of my car and inside before her mother spotted us and freaked out about me driving her home.

But she'd given me the Bureau of Corporations and Charitable Organizations to go on.

At least that was something.

# Chapter Twelve

THE BUREAU OF CORPORATIONS and Charitable Organization's website wasn't hard to find. Hunch was as interested as I was, sitting on his haunches beside me on a kitchen chair.

"We're finally going to find out who would start a company in Cooper's name," I told him as I tried to navigate all of the small print on the government website. The more I thought about it, the more convinced I became that Cooper couldn't have done it on his own. Finally, I found a tab called BUSINESS ENTITY SEARCH. "That must be it," I said as I clicked on the link and it brought me to a searchable database.

It made me feel better to at least have my cat to talk to. I'd made a therapy list about the whole situation while I waited to hear back from Dr. Harrison, but I felt as though cat therapy was having a better effect to calm me—or at the very least, Hunch kept me from letting my anxiety ratchet out of control.

I typed in the address on Marsh Avenue from my photo of the title deed and then waited as a little circle turned in the middle of the screen, letting me know it was working. I stared at the address, wondering where, exactly, in Honeysuckle Grove it was located. I supposed I could look it up on Google Maps. Better yet, as I thought of it, I opened Google Earth in a new tab and typed the address into there.

Google Earth was speedy, considering it cataloged every address in the world, and a second later, it found the address and displayed a bird's-eye view of a suburban-looking neighborhood. From above, it looked like it could be any neighborhood in town, including this one, and the lot in question had a small ranch-style house on it.

I zoomed in but couldn't make out much of the actual house, as a lot of trees shaded it from above. It was a light blue shade of paint and had a small yard in the front and a larger one in back, but both were crowded with trees. The houses on either side of it were yellow. If I changed the angle to 3D mode, I could see a little more—a front walkway similar to mine, with a few cement steps up to a front door. A gate led to a fenced backyard that was too tree-covered to see anything at all.

Hunch pawed at the screen, as if he might be able to move the tree branches out of the way. I wished I could do that, too.

It didn't look any different from any house in any neighborhood. It most certainly did not look like it housed a corporation.

I tabbed back over to the corporations' database and then sucked in a breath because the owner of the Cooper Beck LLC had loaded.

Pirro Klytaimnestra.

I stared at the screen with my mouth open because I knew that name. "This is the same guy who once tried to set up a fake website and impersonate Cooper!" I whispered to Hunch. Then I scrolled through the little bit of other information it offered. The filing and effective date for the company was less than three months before Cooper's death. "Why would this Pirro guy try to set up a corporation to impersonate Cooper right before he died and right in our hometown?"

It was as if this Pirro guy *knew* Cooper was going to die.

This felt creepier than all of Cooper's murder mystery novels.

# Chapter Thirteen

DR. HARRISON COULD FIT me in the next day, but all my therapy lists and explaining away only seemed to bring up more questions.

If this Pirro guy was only a fan, why would he care about setting up a corporation in Cooper's name? And why right before he died? If the timing was purely coincidental, had he bought a property right here in Honeysuckle Grove purely to spy on Cooper? And why open a corporation at all—unless he somehow wanted to try and undercut Cooper's royalties for his already published books? Mitch Reynolds was one of the biggest and most highly respected New York agents, and he was still in charge of making sure Cooper's royalties were forwarded to me after taking his cut. I trusted him not to let a fan meddle with Cooper's money.

Still, just in case, I drafted another email to Mitch. His secretary had said he had no idea about an LLC in Cooper's name, and he hadn't been a part of creating one, but I sent a reply to both Mitch and his secretary, letting them know to be on the lookout for the LLC or its owner, and if he ever came across the name Pirro Klytaimnestra, please let me know as soon as possible.

When the email was sent and I'd written everything I could think of about the situation down to discuss with Dr. Harrison the next day, it was not even dinnertime and I had no idea what to do with myself.

The doorbell rang, but it only turned out to be a delivery guy, dropping off my new magnetic signs for the food truck. I opened them at the kitchen table and showed them to Hunch, but I didn't get the enthusiastic response I was looking for.

Suddenly, I stood, making Hunch jump a little on his chair. "I'm going to take the food truck out," I said on a whim.

I had all of the supplies, and I couldn't just sit here stewing about an investigation that had left me with more questions than answers. Besides, maybe getting out and talking to people in town would help me learn something. Or, at the very least, it might make me feel as though some of the locals might have my back.

As I whipped a big bowl of cream and loaded it along with my fresh bins of berries into the food truck and then attached my magnetic signage, it quickly became clear that Hunch wanted to come along. He pawed at the cab door on the passenger side of the truck.

I sighed. "We just got our health permit, Hunchie," I told him in my most apologetic voice. "Do you know how many violations I'd get with an animal in the kitchen?"

But he looked up at me with what I could only describe as sad, droopy eyes, and I couldn't do it. I couldn't leave him at home.

It was a balmy sixty-five degrees out. As I drove down my street toward the downtown core, I told Hunch, "I'm only planning to stay for the dinner rush." Just long enough to get my mind off all my questions. "I'll leave the windows open, but you'll have to stay up here in the cab."

I wondered about putting him on a leash outside in the future when the weather got too hot to keep him in the front of a vehicle, but I doubted he'd have much patience for that, and what if a dog wandered by?

I parked along the curb in the downtown square near the Town Hall. All the government businesses were closing or closed by that time, but nearly a dozen businesses were still open—coffee shops, eateries, a nail salon, and a sporting goods store, to name a few.

By the time I had the grill warmed up, batter mixed, and my window open, it was nearly six o'clock and there was noticeably less foot traffic outside. I hoped I hadn't missed my window of opportunity.

I skipped outside and wrote on the side board of the truck: "1. Savory prosciutto and gruyere cheese crepe and 2. Fresh berry and cream dessert crepe."

Hopefully, Amber would be around to help with a more creatively descriptive menu soon, but this would have to do for tonight. I'd just finished writing the second option when a couple of ladies left the nail salon and headed my way.

"Oh, this is much better than rushing home to make dinner," one of them said. "Do you have to-go containers?"

I cringed. I hadn't thought of that. But I did have tinfoil. I told them that, and they agreed to buy four of the savory option if I could wrap them to get them home.

By the time I'd finished cooking and wrapping their crepes, another couple arrived, already having had dinner but ready for a dessert crepe to share. I tried to hold a conversation while I assembled their crepe, but it was much more difficult than carrying on a conversation with Amber in my kitchen.

By the time I was done with that, Marv and Donna Mayberry left an office down the way and headed in my direction. "Hi!" I called out. "Can I make you a crepe?"

Donna's face lit up, and she pulled Marv toward my truck. He started to pull out his wallet as she read the options on the board, but I shook my head.

"Put your wallet away. These ones are on the house." It was easier to hold a conversation with people I already knew, and as I worked, I told them how this was my first day out in town with the truck.

"The important thing is that you find a regular location and regular hours and keep to them," Donna told me. "You'll have a following in no time."

Her husband was the advertising expert, but Donna was outspoken and he never challenged her thinking—at least never that I had seen.

"I'd like to chat more about that with Amber before I set any roots." I passed them each a savory crepe and got to work assembling two dessert ones. "But I'm sure we'll figure it out."

"Who was Mr. Tall-blond-and-handsome I saw you with last week?" she asked.

I furrowed my brow, even though I knew exactly who she was talking about. She'd seen me and Pete together, getting frozen yogurt. I didn't particularly want to get into that with the town's biggest gossip, but as she started to describe him—right down to the shirt he had been wearing—I realized it was unlikely I was going to get out of the conversation without giving her something.

"Oh, right. Pete." I passed them their dessert crepes on a plate with tinfoil, so they could take them home to enjoy. "He was Cooper's college roommate. He checks in on me once in a while."

"He must do that often?" Donna asked it as a question.

"Maybe once every few months." Hopefully, from that, she'd get the idea there was nothing between us.

She furrowed her brow. "Not last night?"

I shook my head. "The last time I saw him was the night we went for frozen yogurt." I still felt embarrassed about how that evening had ended.

She raised her eyebrows. "Oh. I could have sworn I saw him at the grocery mart on fifth. Does he live nearby, then?"

I shook my head. "You must have him confused with someone. He's from Pennsylvania."

Marv and Donna left soon after that, assuming she'd had Pete mixed up with another out-of-towner she didn't know. I got swamped with dessert customers soon after, but even with a lineup down the street, I couldn't shake the thought that Pete might have come back to town, then decided he was too wounded by my rejection to even stop by and say hello.

# Chapter Fourteen

THE NEXT DAY, DR. Harrison just looked at me with raised eyebrows as I showed her the many pages I'd scrawled out in my therapy notebook—which had been empty less than a week ago.

"The amount you've written, it doesn't cause you concern?" she asked.

I laughed inwardly. Why should I have expected anything different from a therapist than her asking me how *I* felt about all my questions? "Yes, it causes me concern! That's why I was so desperate to move up my appointment!"

She pressed her hands toward the floor in an encouragement for me to calm down. "Why don't you tell me what causes you the most concern from this last week? Is there one area in particular that your mind seems to be spinning out of control?"

I actually felt as though I'd controlled my mind quite well, considering all I'd been learning. I stared at my notebook as she flipped through, skimming my words but not really taking them in.

What was a bigger concern? That I was a possible suspect in some kind of unknown crime or that someone was masquerading under my late husband's name in my hometown? It was impossible to decide, so I took a breath and dove in. "The other day I was driving to Pennsylvania with my friend from the local police department and I ended up finding out some disturbing information."

"Alex Martinez?" she asked, looking over her own notes. I was surprised at her organization, and in comparison, my notes looked like a haphazard stream of consciousness that probably made me appear crazy.

"That's right." I went on to explain how I'd accidentally seen my name in his notes, and when I'd questioned him about it, he told me I was somehow involved in an investigation and me looking at his notes only made me appear guiltier.

"And is there some area you're feeling guilty at the moment?" Dr. Harrison asked.

That wasn't the point, but I humored her and thought about it for a moment before answering. Sure, I probably felt guilty about how my neediness for friends had gotten both Alex and Amber into trouble more than once. But I kept my answer to the topic at hand. "I haven't committed a crime. At least not one that I'm aware of," I told her.

She nodded, and I went on to explain everything I knew about Ron Beckford and his criminal background and Pirro Klytaimnestra and how he'd once impersonated Cooper online and now he held a company under Cooper's name, with a house right in Honeysuckle Grove.

When I finally stopped to take a breath, Dr. Harrison was flipping pages in my notebook with her brow furrowed.

"What?" I asked.

She looked up at me and shook her head. "I don't know that you're overreacting here, Mallory. There's a lot going on, either a very large number of coincidences, or somehow these situations are connected, and I don't like that you're at the center of all of them."

My whole body sagged in relief. At last someone was taking me seriously. "I don't like it, either," I told her.

She took in a breath and let it out slowly. "Have you spoken to Alex again about all of these things you've discovered?"

I shook my head.

"I think you should. Or if he's not receptive, perhaps you should contact another police officer, at least to let them know about your concern over the company in Cooper's name. If it's in Honeysuckle Grove, it seems like something the police should look into."

I was so thankful to hear this from a professional that wasn't in my own head. I nodded fervently in agreement.

She pulled a small pad of paper from her desk and started writing. "Your cortisol must be through the roof. I'm going to write you a prescription to help keep your anxiety in check. If there are so many unanswered questions surrounding your husband's family, plus this impersonator of your husband's, you'll struggle to have peace until you get to the bottom of all of your questions. But, Mallory, I'm serious. You should not be sitting at home on your own with these concerns. Go to the police. Do it today."

I left Dr. Harrison's office with a sense of gratefulness. The last thing I wanted was to be left alone with all of these concerns.

Now it was just a matter of getting Alex to listen to me.

# Chapter Fifteen

I STOPPED BY THE Honeysuckle Grove Police Department on my way home, but both Alex and Steve Reinhart were out working on a case. I wasn't sure who to leave a message for, so I left a message for both of them, saying I wanted to speak to them about a possible stalker named Pirro Klytaimnestra. I'd talk to whoever called me back. I'd tell them everything I was worried about. As far as I was concerned, I had nothing to hide.

When I got home, I tried to get my mind off my questions, but no matter how much I cooked and cleaned, I couldn't get past the fact that this Pirro Klytaimnestra might be just down the street from me. I kept having the urge to get in my car, set the GPS for the address on Marsh Avenue, and just head right over there.

But I'd warned Amber many times about impulsive and dangerous behavior. How would I ever be the good influence she needed if I went off and made my own impulsive and dangerous decisions?

When an hour passed and I hadn't heard from Alex or Steve, then two hours, I pulled up Amber's contact number on my phone and stared down at it. But I couldn't involve her in investigative work, even if it involved me. *Especially* if it involved me.

I called Sasha to see if she wanted to go for lunch, but she was at the dentist and spoke over a wad of cotton to suggest I call our friend and fellow lunch lady Yvette.

I didn't hesitate and clicked right over to her contact number.

"Yvette?" I asked when it sounded as though someone had picked up, but no one actually answered. "Is anyone there?"

A second later, a young child called, "Mommy!" at full decibel without covering the handset. I pulled my cell away from my ear, and by the time I brought it back, Yvette was on the line.

"I was looking for someone to go for lunch with," I said. "Have you eaten?"

"I'm glad you called! We missed you at the last lunch ladies' meetup, Mallory."

In truth, there had been an oversight about inviting me, but I was afraid if I tried to explain this, she'd see through me to just how desperate and lonely I was. "Yes, I missed all of you, too," I settled on.

"We haven't eaten, but I don't have anyone to watch the kids today. Can you do Friday? My mom should be around." Her mom, Lea, was another of the lunch ladies I'd gotten along with. I supposed I could go through the list and try each of them for lunch today, but many of them were a lot older than me, and I felt like I might sooner be able to open up to Yvette.

"What if I brought something by your place?" I suggested. "I was just about to throw together a turkey and Havarti sandwich for myself." It was sort of true. I had been fiddling around the kitchen but hadn't gotten my mind around actually stomaching any food yet.

"If you don't mind the mess, that'd be great!" she told me and then rattled off her address. "Oh, and Tommy is allergic to mushrooms, and Tillie hates tomatoes."

"No mushrooms and tomatoes. Got it! I'll see you shortly."

Making sandwiches was a good distraction for the next twenty minutes, and after I arrived at Yvette's house, the kids were a great distraction through lunch. I knew her twins from children's church, and at first, they seemed delighted about having me in their home. Yvette hadn't been kidding—it looked a little like a tornado had hit—but so did our kids' area at the end of Sunday School each week.

"Look at my picture," Tillie told me, flashing what looked like a finger painting of either a person or a dinosaur, it was a little hard to tell.

"Beautiful colors," I told her. My praise only egged her brother on, though, and he pushed past her to show me his latest artwork, which was more recognizable but also a lot angrier, with a samurai and a knife and what looked like blood splatters all over the page. "Wow!" I said to him. "Do you like samurai soldiers?"

Tommy looked at me like he had no idea what I was talking about.

Yvette explained, "He's going through a phase," and then ran interference as the kids fought over whose artwork was better.

By the end of lunch, Yvette looked exhausted, so I told her to sit down while I cleaned up the dishes. That lasted for about five minutes, and then she was running after her kids again.

I had to admit, after only a little more than an hour at their place, I was tired, too, but at least I had the luxury of going home for a nap.

By the time I got home, though, my mind ricocheted back to all the problems I'd been able to put aside for a short time, and then there was no way I was going to sleep.

I wished there was someone else I could trust to listen to me and give me good advice, especially since Dr. Harrison said I shouldn't be sitting at home alone with my concerns. I briefly considered calling Tanner but then rationalized I shouldn't involve him in something like this when his family was under suspicion and he was going through so much himself.

I clicked over to Pete's number instead and toyed with my phone before finally hitting CALL. As usual, I got his voice mail, but I at least felt grateful to have someone out there who I didn't have to watch my words around.

"Hi, it's me again," I said after the beep. "I know you're probably still screening my calls and not feeling in any hurry to talk to me, but I really need someone to talk to."

I stopped to take a breath, considering how much I should tell him in a voice mail message. I decided to start with the part I was the most freaked out about at the moment and go from there.

Even though the whole ordeal was quite serious, for some reason, when I opened my mouth, my tone came out light and almost playful. "So I'm onto this big mystery, and I could really use your help to figure it out."

As I said the words, it occurred to me that my light tone was probably my subconscious attempt to get things back to casual between the two of us, without making more of my schmaltzy apologies.

"Remember when Cooper had that stalker back in Fox Hills?" I went on. "We thought it was a guy from your writing program, but it turned out to be a fan, a guy named Pirro Klytaimnestra." I left a space, as though his voice mail might respond to me. "So, anyway, I found this house under Cooper's name, it's located right here in Honeysuckle Grove. I'd never heard anything about it from Cooper, so I figured it must have been a clerical error, but when I looked deeper into it, it turns out this Pirro guy—the same guy who used to be Cooper's stalker—he owns a house under Cooper's name!"

I took a breath, trying to calm my mix of pep and angst over the subject.

"So weird, right?" I asked his voice mail with forced playfulness as soon as I could pull myself together. "I just thought next time you're in town, maybe we could go by there and see what this guy is all about. Or I can do it on my own. But your dad told Tanner he thought you were on a writing retreat, so I just thought I'd check to see if you're back and have time for a quick visit. Please at least call me back if you're around."

I hung up and let out my breath. But I was proud of myself because I knew Pete would call me back this time.

He, of anyone, would understand the craziness of what I was telling him. He cared too much about me to leave me out on my own if I could actually be in danger.

At least, I was pretty sure of it.

# Chapter Sixteen

MY PHONE RANG WHEN I had my hands covered in flour from a mixed berry pie I was making with the leftover berries from my Crepe Express outing.

I clicked the volume button to answer with my pinky and sent it straight to speakerphone. "I'm so glad you called me back!" It hadn't even been half an hour. I knew I could count on Pete.

But a long pause followed. I opened my mouth, trying to come up with yet another apology, but I didn't know where to start, and when nothing immediately came, a woman's voice sounded through my speakerphone.

"Mallory? Is that you?"

It wasn't my sister, Leslie. I'd know her voice anywhere. It also wasn't Amber.

"Um. Yes?" Maybe it was a catering client. Or one of the lunch ladies. Or someone from the food truck. I tried to put on more of a businesslike tone. "How can I help you?"

"This is Helen." When I still didn't immediately gain recognition, she added, "Helen Montrose."

"Oh! Hi!" I tried to quell my enthusiasm and sound more like an adult than her teenager. "Yes, hi."

"I wondered if you could drop by this afternoon? I have something I want to discuss."

Did her tone sound ominous? I wasn't sure. Still, I wasn't about to decline. "Uh, sure. Yeah. Okay."

After hanging up, I thought of all the questions I should have asked. Was this about Amber? Was she okay? Had Helen found out that I had emailed and texted a couple of times, or driven her home, or that I was under investigation?

An hour later, I rang the two-tone chime at the front door of the Montrose mansion. Helen opened the door quickly, as though she'd been waiting right beside it. She had her hair done in its bouffant style and wore a fitted peach dress, which made me think she'd probably been out or was about to go out. Amber often told me about the version of her mother that stayed in bed all day, but I'd never actually witnessed that version.

"Mallory, come in." Helen swung the door the rest of the way open and immediately pasted on a smile that looked false.

I walked through the door, and my gaze darted in every direction. I didn't see or hear anybody. Amber did most of her schooling online at home these days, but the house was as quiet as a tomb. "Is Amber home?" I asked.

Helen shook her head. "I sent the kids out for a few groceries."

I wondered if the errand was only meant to gain some time to talk to me alone.

This was confirmed when she added, "I hoped to have a word with you without Amber around."

I nodded. "Is she . . . Is everything okay?"

Helen must have seen the concern in my eyes because she placed a hand on my shoulder as she said, "Oh, yes, yes. Not to worry."

She led me toward her front room. Even though I'd witnessed more than one gathering in it, the expensive mahogany and brocade furniture made me think of a room that was never touched, let alone sat in.

But she sat on a sofa, and I sat on the edge on the loveseat across from her. The furniture even felt like it was rarely sat on, and I shifted to try and get comfortable. "So what can I help with?" I asked.

Helen sighed and studied me for a long moment before answering. "I hate to say it, but Amber's been listless lately. No concern for her schoolwork. She goes to bed even earlier than me these days."

Helen had just said Amber was fine. This didn't sound fine. This sounded more like the onset of depression.

But before I could express my concerns, Helen went on. "I'm considering letting her spend some time with you again, on a trial basis, perhaps one night a week to work at this catering business of yours. Something to keep her busy."

Busy probably wasn't what she needed as much as someone to talk to. "How has the counseling been going?" I asked. "Are the two of you still going together?"

Helen appeared uncomfortable by my question, looking away quickly. "I— There's been some changes, and well, I've needed to spend some time on my own there."

I opened my mouth to release some of my anger. I was tired of hearing about Helen Montrose and what *she* needed, especially when her daughter had actually been trying to heal from her grief and move on in her life.

But I caught myself. Only a second ago, Helen had offered to let Amber back into my life, at least to some degree. I didn't want to bite the hand that was feeding me, so to speak.

"Amber's a great girl." I decided to sing Amber's praises, rather than focusing on Helen's deficiencies. "I think cooking was a great outlet for her. I'm glad you see value in it, too."

Helen let out a breath, probably thankful I'd diverted the subject from her and her therapy needs. "But, listen. This is only a trial. I don't want Amber spending all her time at your house and forgetting about her family again. That won't work. If all goes well, we can talk about her visiting you more, but for right now, I'm just talking about the odd event with your catering business and no investigative work. Understood?"

I nodded, again holding in everything I wanted to reply.

"If it doesn't go well and Amber won't listen to me or doesn't want to spend any time at home, I'll bring the trial to a quick end." Her words sounded threatening, but I did my best to paste on a smile and be thankful for what she was offering.

Now it was only a matter of getting us another catering gig, so we'd have something to work on together. I was going to do everything in my power to play by the rules.

I left with new motivation to put our business into motion.

# Chapter Seventeen

WHEN I GOT BACK home, Pete's old Ford truck was in my driveway and Pete stood at the front door, ringing the bell. He turned toward the street just as I pulled into my driveway.

I was so happy to see him, I leaped out the driver's door when I barely had my car into park. "Hi! You're here!" I tended to state the obvious when I got excited.

He shrugged. "Yeah, I got your messages. Sorry, I've been pretty busy."

I waved a casual hand as I unlocked the door and let him inside. "I totally understand. I'm just glad you're here now."

At our voices, Hunch padded into the entryway to see who was here. He sniffed the air twice and turned for the kitchen and likely his food dish.

"Your dad thought you might be at a writing retreat?" I said, trying to take the pressure off how many times I had called and whether or not my persistence had made him uncomfortable. "I want to hear all about it."

Pete scratched the back of his neck. "Actually, I wasn't. I was just helping a buddy of mine in Northern Pennsylvania and didn't want to mention it to my dad." I looked at him, confused as to why he'd hide something like that from his dad, but then he went on to explain. "He needed some wiring fixed in his house. Dad would have wanted it to go through the company, but he's a friend, so . . . "

That made sense. From everything I'd heard about Pete's dad, he was a stoic man with hard and fast rules when it came to the construction business he'd built from the ground up. Back in college, Pete used to tell us about how his dad had fired workers for talking about the projects they were working on or for taking two extra minutes on their lunch breaks.

"Nice of you to help your friend," I said, feeling more relieved than I would have expected that Pete had truly been busy and not simply ignoring me. But I had hoped the part about him writing again was true. "So just helping with some wiring? That's all you've been up to?"

He led the way to my living room. It was almost eight o'clock, and I assumed he had already eaten. "Believe me, it's enough. Now tell me about this stalker of Cooper's you think is around again?"

I told him all the details about what I'd found at the title deeds office and then through the Bureau of Corporations and Charitable Organizations. I didn't tell him I'd gotten the tip about the title deeds office by snooping in a police file that had my name in it. I wanted to figure out more about what that was about before I started putting thoughts of illegalities regarding Cooper or me in people's heads.

"And so this Pirro Klytaimnestra was really listed as the owner of a company in Cooper's name?" Pete sounded as flabbergasted as I had been, and for the first time in what felt like a while, I didn't feel crazy.

"That's exactly right."

"And he owns a house right here in Honeysuckle Grove?" When I confirmed this, Pete didn't wait for any more details. He stood and said, "Get me the address. I need to check this out."

"I want to go, too." I wasn't about to let Pete go alone. If he was with me, I certainly felt safe enough.

"You sure you should, Mal?" he asked.

I didn't entertain him with an answer and just headed for my purse and shoes at the door.

"You know, if you're coming, maybe we should take your car." I was glad he wasn't arguing with me about coming along, but I looked at him in question. "It's quieter than my beast," he explained.

It was, and it was also more comfortable, which became important when we got to the house and found it dark. Pete went to the front door, rang the doorbell, and knocked, but didn't get any answer.

"I think we should hole up here," he said, getting back into the driver's seat. "See if anyone comes back."

"Thank you. This means a lot to me."

"We can stay all night if you want to. I don't have to be back in Pennsylvania until tomorrow night."

I smiled over at him. "I really am sorry if I did anything to hurt our friendship, you know, last time you were here. I've missed you, Pete."

He flashed the kind of easy smile that I hadn't seen in over a year. "It's forgotten. And I've missed you, too."

He reached over and squeezed my forearm. I recognized it as a careful move that he wouldn't want to be taken the wrong way. I figured it would take a while for us to get completely back to normal, but I was just glad he was here.

"If we can't have Coop, at least we have each other, right? Don't worry, Mal. I don't want to lose that any more than you do."

I put my seat back a notch and turned to face him. "It's been hard, getting over him. I mean, I don't think I'll ever completely get over him, but finally, I'm at least moving forward and feeling like I want to live again."

Pete smiled a sad smile at that. "Remember the time the three of us snuck into the culinary arts kitchen in the middle of the night because you had this sudden *need* to bake your grandmother's brownie recipe for Coop?"

I laughed. "You're the one who ate three-quarters of the pan. Besides, it's not easy being an aspiring chef and living in student housing without a kitchen, you know?"

It felt good to reminisce about Cooper with Pete, and he went on to recount several other stories I'd forgotten about from our college years.

No cars came or went from the Cooper Beck LLC house, but Pete and I ended up talking for most of the night.

"Do you think this Pirro guy could be away somewhere, like out of town?" I asked when it was just starting to get light out again.

Pete shrugged. "Or maybe it's just a holding place. Maybe he doesn't actually live here."

I had to admit, that thought relieved me some. Although, why buy a "holding" place in the town where I lived, unless he planned to do *something* with it?

"I'm just glad I have you around to help me figure this out. Well . . . " I checked my watch. "At least until tonight."

He smiled wryly. "Actually, I probably should get on the road fairly soon. I'm still wide awake now, but I'm going to need a few hours' sleep before I have to work later."

"You have to work tonight?" Even with my tiredness, my voice showed my shock. Why had I kept him here to watch an empty house all night when he had to work later?

He shrugged. "Yeah, Dad took a contract on a reno that wants to stay open during the day and get the work done through the nights. Believe me, none of us are too happy about it." He glanced at me. "Unless . . . "

"Unless, what?"

"Unless you're scared," he said in a rush. "I don't want to leave you here if you're worried, Mallory, and I don't know, I could talk to my dad and maybe he'd give me a few more days—"

"No way, Pete! Not on your life. You've already been too good to me, sticking around through the night to stake out this house. I'll be fine." In truth, I was much more relaxed, having seen the suburban house with my own eyes. It really didn't look like it held a lot of threatening mystery. Pete looked like he was still unconvinced, so I added in my most confident tone, "Besides, I'm not planning on coming near here again on my own. I'll keep my doors at home locked, and if I'm really scared, you're only a phone call away, right?"

He took a big breath and let it out before answering. "I suppose."

"For now, why don't you get a couple hours' sleep at my place before getting on the road?"

He started my car and put it in drive. "Like I said, I'm pretty wide awake." He drove for several minutes in companionable—or maybe just tired—silence before adding, "I'm glad you called me about this. I hope you always feel like you can come to me with any problems or concerns. You know you can count on me as a friend, right, Mallory?"

I nodded. I did know that.

"Did you know I used to have a bit of a crush on you when we first met, before you started dating Cooper?"

That was a really short time, but I didn't challenge him on it. I could sense he'd liked me a little even when Cooper and I were together, but that had faded quickly when he'd met Eve from my college dorm and they'd gone out for a while.

"It was probably just the memory that made me lean in to kiss you the other night, but you shouldn't worry. I know how things are and how you're not ready to be with anyone else, anyway."

I nodded, feeling guilty because I actually *had* been considering dating Alex before he became so busy. Lately, I'd felt hurt that he was shutting me out, but at the same time, I was still fairly confident he was trying to prove my innocence. That said, he hadn't been there for me lately, and did I still care for him in that way? Could I even trust my own feelings anymore?

"I wonder if there'd be a way to get my detective friend Alex over to the house on Marsh Avenue to take fingerprints." I wasn't completely sure if I was trying to purge myself of my guilt or punish myself by bringing Alex up, but Pete only scoffed at my suggestion.

"I don't think this is worth bothering your detective friend with." He drove for another long minute, wringing his hands on my steering wheel, telling me without saying it out loud that he didn't think I should be spending time alone with Alex.

I tried to decide if it was worth mentioning that Dr. Harrison had thought this was worth sharing with the police. But Alex hadn't called me even once since our car ride to Pennsylvania, not even to return my message from earlier today.

After another long minute, Pete sighed and said, "Look, Mallory, if you're really worried about this, I know a guy. A private investigator. Why don't I give him a call and see when he could stop by and take a few prints? With the police, they have to have warrants and reasons to get warrants. It's all one big headache. My guy can get in and out without anyone even knowing he was there. Let me take care of this for you, okay?"

"That would be amazing. Thank you, Pete. Really."

He looked over and grinned a tired grin. Happy-go-lucky Pete was back, and I was glad. I wouldn't want to leave another conversation wondering when I'd ever hear from him again.

# Chapter Eighteen

THE SECOND AMBER'S MOM gave her permission, Amber went on a dozen online message boards and Facebook groups and had our next catering gig lined up for only two days later.

Thankfully, that took my mind off the house on Marsh Avenue, even if I couldn't seem to stop myself from driving by it a few times a day. Each time I did, it appeared as vacant as it had when I'd been there with Pete.

Tonight's catering job was in a yoga studio that had just opened up not far from the downtown core. I wasn't sure if Honeysuckle Grove would support such a business, but the owner, Cassie May, seemed friendly enough on the phone and had wanted to make a big splash on her opening night. She was planning to sample some of her own fruit smoothies at the event and wanted us to provide healthy appetizers to accompany them.

Amber, as always, had done the research and come up with a dozen recipes for me to choose from, and I forced her to catch up on schoolwork while I did the shopping.

After that, we were cooking together in my kitchen again at long last.

"I've missed this," I told her honestly.

"Uh-huh." It was the most sugary response I could expect from her. I suspected she was put off by Hunch's snubbing of her since she'd walked in the door. Amber and Hunch used to be the best of besties, but it didn't take much to waver

Hunch's trust meter. He sat on his haunches near his food, watching Amber but not coming close or rubbing against her legs as he always used to. "These almond-flour brownies had a four-point-nine-star rating. I can't wait to try them," she said, as though unbothered.

But she didn't fool me. She'd missed Hunch and even me, too. I prepared two large fruit and vegetable platters while she pulled the falafel bites out of the oven to make room for the brownies.

"How's school going?" It was all I could do not to tell her about all the drama that had been going on in my life.

She shrugged. "Same ol'. Biology is a ton of work, and I don't think I'll remember any of it anyway. How about you?" When I didn't answer right away, she added, "You said you made an appointment with Dr. Harrison? Did you like her?"

I had to tread carefully here. "Yeah, I really did. She's been helping me work through some stuff. You know, with Cooper and all that."

She nodded. At least when it came to Cooper, I was pretty sure she wouldn't push.

We kept busy discussing our recipes, which were all new to us, and before long, it was time to pack up the food truck and go. As we hauled bin after bin toward the truck, though, Hunch saw this as his cue to follow us outside and paw at the door of the front cab.

I sighed. "Hunch, you'd be stuck in there for hours."

It was a cool night, but I still didn't see the point of him coming along if he wouldn't be able to leave the cab.

"I can check on him." Amber came up behind Hunch, swiped him up, and looked him in the eyes. I'd never dare to hold my cat within claws' reach of my face, but even after all this time apart, Amber clearly trusted him. "What do you say, Hunchie?"

And a second later, Hunch purred in response. Sure, he could hold a grudge with me and anyone else in this world for months, but never with Amber.

Cassie May's Yoga Studio didn't look like much from the street, but once through the front doors, I could tell she had put a lot of money into the place. It made sense why she wanted to get as many locals through the door as possible to see it.

The bulk of the studio was one big open room with hardwood floors and giant windows along the back wall, facing out onto a greenbelt. Purple yoga mats formed a sunburst in the middle of the room, and high tables sat sporadically around the rest of the space. A young woman of about thirty-five stood at the far end behind a white juice bar, blending drinks in a blender, and didn't hear us come in at first. Amber and I headed straight for her, and as soon as her blender stopped, she looked up to see us.

"Oh, hi! Mallory?" She looked between us.

I was carrying a warming tray. I set it down on her counter and held out a hand. "That's right. Cassie May?"

She smiled brightly. "I'm glad you're a little early. I thought you could set up a combo plate on each table and then the bulk of the food here at the juice bar. What do you think?"

It was an open house where all in town were invited to come and check out the space, take a free introductory yoga class if they wished, and enter into drawings for free workout gear and memberships. If not for Amber, I probably wouldn't have had the extra plates to divvy up our appetizers for each table, but thankfully, Amber had a pretty good handle on being overprepared at this catering gig. We had invited her mom. I hoped she would show up and see just how capable Amber was.

Cassie May was a big ball of energy and skipped back and forth between mixing smoothies, setting up mats and towels, turning on music, and greeting guests once they began to arrive. With Amber's help, we had gotten the food laid out in almost no time.

"I like the new food truck," she told me when we finally stopped to take a breath on two of the stools behind the juice bar. "Next job'll be to convince Mom to let me work on that once a week."

Apparently, Helen Montrose had turned her nose up when Amber first suggested that if we didn't book any catering gigs right away, we could set the truck up downtown.

Amber's face lit up with an idea. "Hey, maybe we could set up in our driveway sometime!" My face must have shown my confusion, so she went on. "You'd have to do all the prep work on your own, shopping and everything, but then once you're parked, I'll ask my mom if I can go into the truck to make her a fancy crepe. I'll bet if she sees our idea in action, rather than just hearing about it, she'd be more receptive."

I tilted my head, thinking about it. "You know, it's not a bad idea."

"I know!" she said, the overconfident teenager she always was. She popped off her stool. "Speaking of the food truck, I'm going to check on Hunch."

A couple of dozen people had arrived already, so while Amber was gone, I made my way around the room with a tray of food, introducing myself or chatting with the ladies I already knew. Lea and Yvette had shown up from my lunch ladies group, and of course, Donna Mayberry was not about to miss a local social event.

"What kind of cases are you working on with that handsome policeman of yours?" Donna nudged me in the arm and then went on to explain to the gossip posse surrounding her that I regularly helped handsome Alex Martinez solve local crimes.

"Well, not exactly," I hedged. "I mean, I used to help out when I could, but really that's a job for our local trained police force." A shame I couldn't explain washed over me as I said the words.

"Mallory has all the best-looking men around town wrapped around her little finger. You should see the blond I saw her with the other day," Donna said. The ladies with her leaned in closer, clearly taken in by Donna's story. "Mallory says he doesn't visit often, but I could swear I've seen him around town once or twice, so I think I know differently," she practically singsonged.

Thankfully, before the other ladies could comment on this unwarranted rumor, the door across the room opened, and Helen Montrose walked through with her son, Seth.

"Excuse me," I said, setting down my empty tray and walking toward them. After I'd greeted them both, I realized I probably should have feigned busyness until Amber had reappeared.

"Where's my daughter?" Helen asked without so much as a hello, scanning the wide, open room.

"Oh, she's just outside in the food truck," I said slowly, as if that might buy me a little time. I feared if I spelled out that she was looking in on my cat, Helen might erupt with an argument about how she hadn't suggested our reuniting so her daughter could cat sit.

"Probably getting more supplies, right?" Seth filled in the blank.

I was liking that kid more and more each time I saw the way he looked out for his little sister. With his raggedy auburn hair and tattered jeans, he may not have looked the part of a responsible, caring brother, but he sure acted it.

"That's right," I said, not missing a beat. "She'll be back in any minute. While you wait, you should definitely try her almond-flour brownie bites."

I led them toward the nearest table. I knew from Amber that her mother had a serious sweet tooth. She usually avoided carbs at almost all costs—unless something indicated the treats might be a healthy and lower carbohydrate alternative.

"Oh, maybe just one." She helped herself from the plate almost before I'd finished speaking.

Unlike his mother, Seth inhaled most of what was left on the plate in about three seconds. Back when we used to cook together regularly, Amber had told me whenever she brought food home her brother barely let her get it in the door before he swiped it out of her hands.

"Come and try a smoothie as well." I picked up the empty plate to refill and led the way to the juice bar. In truth, I was just stalling, but thankfully, it worked because, by the time I'd served them both a portion of smoothie, Amber reappeared, washing her hands in the juice bar sink.

"You came!" Amber didn't get a lot of parental attention, and so when her mom did make an effort, Amber went out of her way with enthusiasm about it.

"The brownies are excellent." Helen reached for another from my newly stocked plate. I didn't have the heart to tell her how much coconut oil was in them. "I understand you made them, sweetie?"

Amber beamed. Then she proceeded to take over entertaining her mother and brother, and I made my way around the room again, introducing myself to those I hadn't met. Soon Cassie May took over with her introductory yoga class, and the evening progressed like a well-oiled machine.

By the time she closed the doors on her open house and Amber and I had cleaned up, I was exhausted. Cassie May still looked like she could run a marathon, spurred on by the evening's success.

Helen Montrose had only stayed for half an hour, and I promised I would drive Amber home before midnight. Their mansion was a few miles up the mountain from here, not far at all. What also wasn't far, though, was Marsh Avenue, and with our catering event behind me, that was all I could think about as we packed the last of our serving supplies into the food truck

"Hey, listen, it's earlier than I thought. Do you mind if I just drop something off at a friend's house on our way to your place?"

Amber shrugged, distracted by Hunch in the passenger seat, soaking up the love he'd held back from her earlier. "Sure. What do you have to drop off?"

I thought fast. "That silver tray we used for the cupcakes? I saw it at her place the other day and asked if I could borrow it." In truth, I'd purchased the silver tray last week when Amber hadn't been around, so she wasn't familiar with it.

She shrugged again, so I got on the road and headed toward Marsh Avenue. As I drove closer, my hands gripped the steering wheel tighter to keep them from shaking.

*There's probably nobody even there*, I told myself. There hadn't been every time I'd driven by so far. But somehow coming here at night, without Pete to protect me, felt a lot scarier.

I pulled up to the curb across the street from the house, and even though there were no vehicles in the driveway and the house was mostly dark as it had been each time before, it looked as though a faint light might be shining from inside the back of the house. Or maybe it was just a reflection from a streetlight.

"Is that your friend's house?" Amber asked, almost making me jump. I'd momentarily forgotten she was beside me.

"Oh. Uh. Yeah. But it doesn't look like she's home."

"It's almost eleven o'clock," Amber said, all casual. "Maybe she's in bed. Why don't you just leave it on her back porch or something?"

"I—uh—good idea." As I got out of the cab and went to retrieve my new silver platter from the back of the food truck, I told myself over and over again that this wasn't a good idea. I shouldn't be investigating this house without Pete or even Alex around.

Then again, I had to act casual or Amber would know something was up, and she'd for sure want to be involved and demand to know everything.

But the driveway was empty, I reminded myself again. It was probably just a reflective streetlight. I emerged from the back of the food truck and pasted on a casual smile as I passed the cab, but Amber's attention was rapt on my cat.

I looked both ways and crossed the street. As I soft-stepped closer to the house, I thought about my plan. I'd just go far enough around the side of the house to stash the tray some-where. It had been forty dollars, but I didn't really care about the money. I could buy another one.

Then I'd go back to Amber and we'd drive on to her house. If I was really concerned, I could call Pete later and ask after his private investigator friend.

But when I got to the other side of the road and closer to the house, I could tell the light was not a reflection from a streetlight. A blue-ish light shone from somewhere deep inside.

I aimed to stick to my plan, but as I rounded the side of the house, I couldn't seem to stop myself from going farther and farther until I was at the back corner. I peered around the corner, and sure enough, the blue light shone through a back sliding glass door.

The trees in the backyard made it feel secluded. I placed the serving tray gently at my feet and then edged a little closer until I was behind a shrub near the back patio. I couldn't see much inside besides a simple fold-out table and some folding chairs in what looked to be a dining room. On the table sat several books strewn about, but I couldn't see the titles of any of them. A laptop was open, facing away, and that was the source of the blue light I'd seen from the front yard. And beside the laptop . . . a coffee cup.

Someone had been here—and recently. The laptop screen was still on, which led me to believe this someone might still be inside.

At the thought, I sucked in a breath and quick-stepped all the way back to the corner of the house. As I turned to run back for the front yard, my foot caught the silver serving tray I'd forgotten all about, and it made a loud clank against the cement path.

I held in my shriek, left the tray to settle its own clatter, and raced toward the front yard and my food truck. It wasn't until I was inside the front cab that I let out my breath in a gust.

Amber raised an eyebrow at me. "What has you so spooked? Did you see a raccoon? Or a bear?"

Amber was as good at coming up with reasonable explanations as her brother.

I nodded and did my best to take a breath and paste on a smile. "I don't know what it was. But it was something."

# Chapter Nineteen

I SPENT THE ENTIRE next day baking in hopes of making myself forget the house on Marsh Avenue and its possible occupant. I'd left messages for Alex, Steve, and Pete, but none of them were calling me back.

Just before eight in the evening, I was about to sit down and scroll through Netflix when a sudden knock at the door and then the doorbell made me jump.

I crept toward the front door, but the side window panel showed it was only Alex. He hadn't called back, but I was thankful he'd come by in person.

Usually, I didn't even lock my door until I went to bed at night, but today, I'd locked both the door lock and the deadbolt above, which was difficult to turn and it took me a moment to get it unlocked for Alex.

As soon as I got the door open, he looked between the deadbolt and my face with a raised eyebrow. "Have you been watching those horror movies again?" When we drove to Pennsylvania, I'd mentioned that it was the only genre where I hadn't already seen everything a million times. He hadn't argued with me then about it, but now he asked, "Do you really think that's a good idea to watch that stuff alone?"

I felt like saying I wouldn't be alone if he had more time for me! He didn't trust me enough to talk to me, and he criticized me for emailing Amber. Now he was criticizing me for watching horror movies on my own? Why couldn't he trust me to make any good choices? Didn't he know how hard I was trying?

But was that the way I wanted to start this conversation?

I looked past him toward his car. "No Hunter?"

Alex sighed. "He's in his carrier. I figured I could tie him up in your backyard if you don't mind, so we can talk for a few minutes?"

I wasn't about to argue with this. I told him I'd heat up some of my leftover stew for him while he got his dog settled. Hunter yelped a few times, clearly not enjoying being tied up, and Hunch growled at one of the rear windows off the kitchen. He was all growl and no action—as if he was about to confront a dog and do anything about it.

As I waited for Alex's stew to heat in its pot, I pulled some vegetables from the fridge for a salad to accompany it. As I worked, I peeked through my kitchen window. Hunter had stopped yelping, and Alex was squatted to meet him at eye level.

He spoke to the dog, and I almost thought I could see Hunter nodding in response. When Alex stood again and headed for the sliding glass door I'd left unlocked for him, Hunter let out a small whine but then lay down on my pad of back patio cement and put his head on his paws.

If that dog wasn't so busy keeping Alex away from me, I'd have to admit he was quite adorable.

Of course Hunch did not think so. Not one bit. The second Alex walked through the glass door, he took one sniff and his back moved into a high arc.

"Hey, Hunch," Alex said. "It's okay, it's only me."

But when Alex took a step closer toward my cat, he let out a loud hiss and darted out of the room.

"I suppose I've brought the enemy into his lair, haven't I?" Alex watched after where Hunch had disappeared. "Too bad. That little tabby was starting to grow on me."

"He'll get over it," I said as I scooped some stew into bowls for both of us. I didn't know if that was true. But I'd seen evidence of Hunch forgiving Amber pretty quickly, so who knew?

After I placed our food on the table, a long silence passed between us. Sure, Alex was eating, and maybe he wasn't uncomfortable in the least. But me? My sweaty fingers fumbled over one another under the table as I tried to settle on one of the many things I wanted to talk over with Alex—and which one might be the least likely to push him out the door.

I decided on the house on Marsh Avenue. That, of anything, shouldn't push him away, and although a lot of issues were keeping me awake at night these days, that one seemed the most threatening.

"Remember how I found that property on the comptroller website in Cooper's name?" I asked.

Alex stopped chewing and looked up at me. I immediately felt as though I'd chosen the wrong topic to start with. To try and cover, I quickly rambled on, racing through the details of visiting the title deeds office and then finding out the owner of the house was the same guy who had once stalked Cooper.

"My friend Pete—Cooper's college roommate?—he's been helping me look into it a bit."

"Pete Kline?" Alex asked, looking down and taking another spoonful of stew.

I didn't remember ever telling Alex Pete's last name. Had I and just forgotten about it? Or was Alex aware of it because of his investigations into me and Cooper? "That's right."

Alex shook his head. "Don't bother Pete with it. No need for him to drive all the way into town. Just give me the address. I'll look into it."

I should probably have been thankful, but something about this conversation was making me uneasy. First of all, it had been days since I'd left a message about a possible stalker, and Alex hadn't exactly rushed over here to ask me about it. Besides, his suggestion felt more like a directive than a casual remark. Was Alex jealous of Pete? If so, I was glad I hadn't told him about the time Pete almost kissed me or the night we'd spent in my car, staking out the house on Marsh Avenue.

I decided to leave this subject alone for the moment. "Look, I know you're working on a case to do with Cooper's uncle Ron, and maybe Cooper, and maybe even me. I talked to Cooper's parents. I know you're not supposed to tell me anything, but if I can help in any way, I want to, and I swear, if I did anything wrong, I never meant to, and I'll pay the price, whatever it is."

Alex looked sidelong at me as he finished his last bite of stew. Then he took in a long breath and blew it out. "Okay. I shouldn't be telling you this, but you are currently under investigation for some shady business dealings Steve believes are connected to Cooper and his uncle, Ron Beckford."

I furrowed my brow and nodded as seriously as I could, even though that seemed as though it had to be a joke.

He pushed his bowl aside, opened his briefcase, and pulled out a file. He flipped it open inside his briefcase, likely shielding it from my nosy gaze. Finally, he lifted an eight-by-ten photo onto the table. "Have you ever seen this man?"

The man had to be in his fifties, dark-skinned with graying sideburns and a thick afro.

I shook my head. "No. I'm pretty sure I'd remember him. But, no."

Alex nodded. Then he showed me a photo of a woman who looked almost as masculine in the face as the man in the first photo did, but she wore hoop earrings and a blouse with lace at the neck.

Again, I shook my head with no recollection. "Who are they?"

"That's Ron and Doreen Beckford," Alex told me, slipping the photos back into his briefcase. "They've been separated for a number of months, but we have reason to believe they still may be involved in a crime ring together."

"Crime ring? Like . . . the mafia?"

Alex chuckled under his breath. "Nothing quite that big and organized. But it seems there is a fair bit going on under the surface. From what we've discovered so far, Cooper may have been involved, and this house you've discovered on Marsh Avenue—we were already aware of it, and it may be involved, too."

"Does that mean Ron Beckford and Pirro Klytaimnestra are working together?"

"Possibly," Alex said. "It seems Doreen Beckford may have been impersonating you."

Impersonating *me?* But she looked nothing like me. "Why would she do that? *How* would she do that? Have you figured out where these people are? Are they here in town? If Doreen Beckford has been impersonating me, does that mean Pirro is impersonating Cooper again?"

"I can't tell you any more about it, Mallory. Not right now." He looked at me with serious eyes. "But I need you to stay away from that part of town."

I had no problem with that. It still frustrated me that he was shutting me down and not trusting me, but my hope, from the expression in his dark eyes, was that he was taking this all serious enough and I didn't have to worry about my own safety as long as I did what he told me. I nodded my agreement.

He read off another list of about five names and asked me if I knew any of them, but I only recognized one: Peter Becker. Of course, I only knew that name because I'd seen it in Alex's notes splayed out on the backseat of his car, so I shook my head and tried my best to look innocent.

"When's the last time you visited Mayhew Bank?"

I squinted, mostly from pain and discomfort. That was the building where Cooper had died. "Not since a little after Cooper's death."

Surprise flickered on Alex's face, but just for an instant. Then it became unmoved. "You don't do your regular banking there?"

I shook my head. "I moved our accounts to the other bank in town shortly after . . . you know."

He nodded and softened. "You moved all of your joint accounts? And what did you do about Cooper's solo accounts?"

I pulled back. "Everything was in both of our names. It was the one thing that I was told was 'easy' about the whole process of dealing with Cooper's estate, even though it sure didn't feel easy."

Again, a flicker of surprise.

"Why?" I had to ask, recalling the account number I'd seen in Alex's notes. I had deleted my photo but jotted down the account number first. "Does this case involving Ron Beckford somehow have something to do with the bank where Cooper died?"

I'd spent months after Cooper's death trying to convince myself that it had been a senseless accident that could only be blamed on old wiring and bad winter weather. I hated that this one conversation with Alex was making me feel as though it wasn't as simple as that again.

So what if Cooper had a secret house and secret accounts? I told myself the words, but I didn't believe their casualness for a second. Besides, I still felt convinced he hadn't had any knowledge of the house on Marsh Avenue.

At least I hoped he hadn't.

"Back when you had accounts at Mayhew Bank, how often would you say you went in there? Often enough to recognize the tellers?" Alex asked, still in the soft tone, but I could tell this was official business and wanted to help if I could.

I shrugged. "No, I rarely went in there. Cooper used to take care of all our banking." I wondered as I said the words if that shed more guilt toward my late husband. I hated the amount of suspicion this was putting on him, without him here to defend himself. "Although, I did stop in there last Monday." I said it to bring the attention away from Cooper and back to me, but I regretted it when Alex's eyes widened at me. I quickly added, "Just to put up a flyer for my catering business with Amber. That's it." Whatever the case, I would be honest about my part of things to get to the truth.

"So you don't have an account under yours or Cooper's name at Mayhew Bank?" he asked again. "And you did not deposit any money when you went in to put up that flyer?"

The repetition frustrated me, and I knew from seeing him with other suspects in other cases that this was one of his methods for catching somebody in a lie. Did that mean he thought I was lying? I'd thought he was trying to prove my innocence, but maybe he really had lost all trust in me. "No. I don't want to bank there. I have no accounts there. I don't know why you keep asking."

He made some notes in his file, but I had the distinct impression he was only avoiding my eyes.

"This Ron Beckford, he's been to prison, right? What has he done?"

I thought Alex could at least tell me that since Rita and Tanner Beck didn't feel the need to keep this information from me, but he only shook his head and said, "Not yet, Mallory."

His phone buzzed from the table. He picked it up, looked at the screen, and stood a second later. "Thanks for your honesty. We haven't gotten to the bottom of this yet, but don't worry, we will. I'll be looking closely at it all and make some sense of it."

As he strode toward the glass door and for his impatient dog who strained against his leash toward the house, I could only hope he was right. Because what else could I do to find out the truth about this whole mixed-up situation?

Later that night as I double-checked all my locked doors, an unfamiliar dark car on the street caught my attention. A man who appeared to be reading on his phone sat in the driver's seat, and yet I felt strangely watched when I looked at him. I didn't recognize the man or the car and wondered if I should call Alex or Pete. Alex was closer, but I wondered if he would only blame my overactive imagination on the movies I'd been watching.

Besides, he had more than enough to worry about these days.

And the more I stood there, without the man looking in my direction even once, the more I thought this one instance *was* only my overactive imagination.

I snapped a photo of the license plate of the car, regardless, then triple-checked my locks and went to bed.

# Chapter Twenty

SURPRISE OF SURPRISES, AMBER stopped by the next afternoon. She must have taken the bus because when I let her in, I didn't see her brother's or her mother's car in the distance. The dark car I'd been concerned about the night before was still parked against the curb across the street, but now it sat empty. The man must have been visiting one of my neighbors.

"Why are your doors all double locked?" Amber raised an eyebrow at me. I'd become a bit more competent in opening the deadbolt since Alex had visited, but Amber had spent the night enough to know I never used both locks.

I waved a hand. "Too many scary movies before bed. But what brings you by?" I glanced toward my closed door. "Does your mom know you're here?"

Amber snickered under her breath. I knew she'd eventually tire of her mother's strict rules. Apparently, today was that day.

"You should text and let her know you stopped by." Now that Helen Montrose had given her a little freedom to see me—on a trial basis, no less—the last thing I wanted to do was mess that up.

She snickered again. "Don't worry your pretty little head about it, Mallory. I'm not staying. I just had to change buses at fourth and thought I'd stop and say hi."

The fourth street bus stop was at the corner, less than a block away. I worked the tension out of my shoulders. "Where are you headed? Do you need a ride somewhere?" I'd come to terms with the fact that if her mother wasn't going to get out of bed to drive her places, that was the least I could do.

She shook her head. "Nah. Bus comes in ten minutes. But thanks." She swooped up Hunch, who had been a little slower to come into the entryway to greet her, possibly wondering if she may have brought a dog along, too. But once he saw—and smelled—that she was canine-less, he immediately started purring.

Then it made sense. Amber wasn't really here to see me.

"So where did you say you were headed?" I asked again, trying not to feel as though no one had time for me.

"I didn't." She shrugged, then a smirk made its way onto her lips. She didn't do coy and secretive well. At least she didn't with me. "Going downtown to run an errand for Alex."

"For Alex?" My eyebrows shot up. "Did he call you and ask you to?"

She shrugged. "I called him." I waited for more, and eventually, she gave it to me. "Mom said I couldn't work on investigations with you, but she never expressly forbid me to help Alex."

I crossed my arms. "So you've still been working with him regularly?" I had to admit, I felt more than a little jilted by being left out of this.

But she shrugged again and said, "Nah. Just the last couple of days. I could hear how busy he was, so I pretty much forced my help on him."

"What have you been doing for him?" I picked at a thread on my sweater sleeve, feeling defensive and wondering how much she knew about the case he was working on involving me and Cooper.

"Eh, just running errands and stuff."

"What kind of errands?" This was starting to feel like an interrogation, but I couldn't help myself.

She rolled her eyes. "Dropping off mail at the post office, picking up packages at the municipal office, that sort of thing. I don't think he's giving me real jobs anyway."

"No?" I tried to hide my relief.

She shook her head. "Like yesterday? He had me help him figure out how to download and open an e-book copy of a novel on his computer and show him how to take notes inside the book app. Then he started reading and not saying a word to me while I took care of his dog."

On the word "dog," Hunch immediately stiffened in her arms and stopped purring.

I guess I shouldn't have been surprised that she'd already met Hunter. She must not have seen him today yet, though, or Hunch would've taken one sniff and left the room.

"And what will you be helping him with today?"

She sighed. "Just dog sitting again. He said he can't get any reading done with Hunter bouncing around his office."

I squinted in confusion. With Alex being so busy, it was unlikely he had time for casual reading. "And you said this was a novel you helped him download?" I asked. When she nodded, I pried further. "What was it called? I'm always looking for a good book."

She twisted her lips, methodically petting Hunch, who had finally let the "dog" comment go and started purring again. "I can't remember the title, but the author was a guy named Peter Becker. I remember it because the last name was so close to yours."

I sucked in a breath and held it, trying not to show that this meant anything to me. I didn't trust myself to speak evenly just yet.

"Anyway, I just wanted to come by and see you and give Hunch a quick hug." She let Hunch down, reached for the door handle, and then looked back at me with a wink. "I won't tell Mom if you won't."

And a second later, she was gone.

# Chapter Twenty-one

AS SOON AS AMBER was down the road, I opened my laptop at my kitchen table and pulled up all of three books listed by Peter Becker on my browser. I read their synopses and they seemed like suspense-filled thriller type stories Alex had been encouraging me to stay away from on Netflix. All of them followed a character named Eddy Kim, a vigilante trying to help bring justice to a town run by a shady police force. The stories sounded interesting enough, if a little predictable. One thing I used to love about Cooper's novels was that even if we had talked over the plot of one of them a hundred times, the twists and turns while reading still took me by surprise.

Even though I suspected Alex was right and this might not be the most appropriate reading material for me while living alone, I purchased all three e-books without hesitation. The third one in the series had only been released a few days prior. They appeared to be self-published, as the publisher was listed as Peter Becker Books on all three. If these novels were by an author who was listed in Alex's investigation notes, I had to figure out why.

The covers of all three books were similar—comparable to most books in the genre, probably. Dim shading, big block lettering, and a different creepy-looking house on each cover. The more I looked at them, the more they made me shiver, and so I stopped staring at the covers and opened the first book in the series to read a little.

The first five pages told me everything I needed to know about the author's writing style. His writing was fast and a bit messy, but he knew his genre and most certainly knew how to create suspense. I was just finishing the first chapter when my oven beeped and made me jump right out of my chair.

I took a breath. It was only the blueberry oatmeal muffins I'd put in before Amber had stopped by. After taking them out of the oven and lifting them onto a cooling rack, I read another chapter while standing at the counter, waiting for them to cool. By the time I checked on them again, though, I must have gotten caught up in reading because they were completely cool to the touch.

When it was time for bed—three-quarters of the way through the first book—I hadn't thought about TV movies even once. I hadn't thought about anything, in fact, since starting to read. If Hunch hadn't meowed at me, I would have probably forgotten to feed him or lock all my doors before bed.

Well, at least this was a reprieve from living in constant fear about people impersonating me and/or Cooper. The dark car was still parked out front, with the man sitting in the driver's seat again on his phone, but even that didn't keep my attention for long. I took the stairs two at a time to my bedroom while I loaded the book to where I'd left off on my phone.

I'd finished the first book by midnight and the second—which went a lot faster once I knew the characters—by three a.m. I should go to sleep, but I had nothing scheduled for the next day, and I figured it couldn't hurt to read a few pages of the third, just to see what it was about.

By six a.m., I still hadn't slept a wink, not able to sleep first because of the tension and then because of the showdown at the end where Eddy Kim starts an electrical fire on the roof of the police headquarters.

All the descriptions of the fire igniting, and the flames enveloping the villainous police chief, and the two other innocent police officers inside the police station where the fire erupted were too familiar from the way Cooper had died.

I felt as though I could see it all happening, but to Cooper rather than the fictitious police chief. Eddy Kim stood across the street, watching the flames, and I felt like I was standing in his shoes, except I was envisioning myself sixteen months ago, watching the bank burn. I hadn't been there. I hadn't had the foreknowledge the way Eddy Kim seemed to have about the police station fire, but otherwise, it felt incredibly familiar. On top of that, it took place in the middle of winter, also like Cooper's accident. I'd always had a feeling something wasn't right about Cooper's death.

The haunting scene with Eddy Kim was stirring up my suspicious hackles again. Why was Alex so interested in this author and these novels? Did he think there was some tie-in to Ron Beckford or Cooper? Could Ron have been involved in Cooper's death somehow? Did Alex think it was a falling-out between thieves, so to speak? But he said I was a suspect. Maybe I was overreacting or making something out of nothing, but could Alex suspect *me* of doing something that had led to Cooper's death?

# Chapter Twenty-two

I SLEPT IN FITS and starts until noon and finally pulled myself out of bed, a wreck from my nearly sleepless night. When I made my way downstairs and saw the dark car still parked across the street with the man inside sipping a coffee, my tired brain decided I needed to call Alex about it right this second.

Could it be Pirro Klytaimnestra or Ron Beckford or one of their accomplices?

For the first time in ages, Alex picked up his phone when I called. I was unprepared to actually speak to him and bumbled over my first words. "Uh, yeah, hi. This car, outside my house. I'm not sure if it's anything you've done, or . . . It's a dark car, and a man's inside it drinking coffee."

Alex cut off my rambling. "You're concerned about a man in your neighborhood drinking coffee?"

"Well, yeah. But he's been there before. And his car's been there for several days." As I said the words out loud, I heard my overreaction. This, of anything, was my mind playing tricks and making me overanxious. Even though I had something legitimately to be concerned about in my life, I couldn't let everything become a bigger concern than it should be.

Alex sighed. "Yeah, okay. I'll come by and have a look as soon as I can." Poor guy sounded exhausted.

"You know, it's probably nothing. I'm sorry I bothered you, Alex." I was embarrassed by my overreaction, this time because of a book, and in an instant decided not to bombard him with the rest of the crazy theories my late-night reading had sparked in me.

"No, no. I want you to be able to call me whenever you're worried about anything." Even though he said the words, he sounded distracted, and I didn't believe him. "Have you heard from your friend Pete?"

Did he sound jealous? I wasn't sure. "Not in a few days, but hopefully he'll be in town again soon."

"I wonder if it's a good idea, you inviting him over to watch movies and all that. Maybe it gives him the wrong idea . . . "

Now it definitely sounded like jealousy. The thought brought a small smile to my face. Even if Alex didn't have time for me, even if I was somehow implicated in a crime he was investigating, he obviously still cared and wanted to prove me innocent. "Don't worry, I'm being careful not to lead him on," I said, wondering if I'd been careful enough. I was glad Pete and I had discussed our friendship, but I did feel somewhat guilty about not being forthright with him about my feelings for Alex.

I should do that. Next time he was in town, for sure.

"Look, just cool it with having him over for the time being, okay?"

I squinted. "No, not okay. Look, I get it if there are things you can't tell me, and I even get it if you're so busy you barely have time to talk, but Pete's a good friend and at least he has time for me."

"I'm just saying you should be careful, Mall—"

"And I'm telling you I am being careful! I'm sorry if you don't trust my judgment, but you're not around enough to know how I'm handling all the decisions in my life. I'm not stupid, Alex. At least Pete cares enough to listen and believes me—"

"It's not a matter of believing you, but—"

"But you don't think I can make good decisions, even about my friends. Yeah, I get it. Thanks anyway, but I won't keep you any longer." With those words, I hung up, my hands shaking.

I stared at my phone for ten minutes, but when he didn't call back, I decided I had to try and put him out of my mind. I made myself a piece of avocado toast and then lay down on the couch for a nap, taking long, slow breaths, trying to let the stress go. Hunch snuggled up in the crook of my legs, and his loud breathing eventually put me to sleep. Even though I didn't think Hunch could protect me in all situations, he had saved my life more than once, and having him at my side definitely helped me to relax.

I awoke with a start when the hum of a garbage truck moved down the street outside. I checked the time on my phone and was pleasantly surprised I'd been out for over three hours. I gently tried to nudge Hunch aside so I could sit up and stretch, but he went from fast-asleep-purr-engine to wide away in about two seconds.

As I sat up, he stood at the base of the couch, staring up at me, like he was waiting for me to tell him what was next on our agenda.

"I'd better see if it's too late to get my garbage to the road," I told my cat.

I padded to the door, wishing I'd thought to put my garbage bin out at the road before lying down on the couch. It turned out it was definitely too late to get my garbage to the road, but when I had my door open, I immediately noticed something else.

The dark car and the coffee-drinking man were finally gone.

I wondered if Alex had come by while I was napping. Or had the man left on his own?

My tired still-waking-up brain kept asking questions as I showered and made a sandwich for a late lunch. Would Alex have come to my neighborhood to check on the car and not stop to say hello? Maybe I shouldn't be surprised after how I'd hung up on him, but at the same time, I was still angry and confused.

Hunch seemed just as full of questions by the time I stood at the sink to wash my lunch dishes. He paced back and forth on the kitchen floor behind me, and I could practically hear him telling me how eager he was to be out and investigating a crime again.

I hated to admit it, but I felt the same way.

"Do you want to drive by Marsh Avenue with me?" I asked my cat, knowing I shouldn't, especially after I'd promised Alex I'd stay away. But I wasn't planning to actually stop. I'd only drive by and see if there were any cars in the driveway or any lights on inside. Maybe it was up to me to prove my innocence.

I'd barely gotten my question out when Hunch padded to the front door and then scratched at it, making his answer more than clear.

# Chapter Twenty-three

HUNCH COULD BARELY SIT still while I drove, hopping into the backseat and looking out all the windows. It was all I could do to concentrate on the road in front of me with his growls and mewls of delight over heading out into an investigation once again.

A drive-by likely wouldn't be enough excitement for my curious cat. As I drove, I had the idea of going by the neighbor's houses on Marsh Avenue to see what they could tell me about the inhabitant of 2388 Marsh Avenue. What could that hurt?

I couldn't go in as a police consultant, not with Alex having forewarned me to stay away, not to mention I was implicated in an investigation at the moment. Instead, by the time I pulled onto the street in question, I decided to drop in as a friend of Pirro Klytaimnestra's. That way, I could also bring Hunch along.

The driveway of the LLC house once again sat empty. I had the urge to go and look for my silver platter along the side of the house but mentally slapped that thought away. I'd just told Alex he should trust me to make good decisions. I would keep my distance.

It was the middle of the day, and although parked cars were dotted all along the curb of Marsh Avenue, there weren't many in driveways. Only one house looked sure to be occupied, with a blue Honda in the driveway and lights on inside.

I parked between it and Pirro Klytaimnestra's house and then turned to Hunch, who still stared out my back window. It surprised me he wasn't looking straight at the LLC house, as Hunch usually had such a strong investigative sense. Plus we'd come by here the other night after our catering gig.

Then again, he'd been lapping up Amber's long-lost affection at the time and probably hadn't cared about who I'd been delivering my silver platter to.

The lady occupant of the house with the Honda answered the door only seconds after I knocked. This made me feel somewhat safer—people in this neighborhood were on alert and most likely would at least call the police if this Pirro guy strutted out his door and started chasing after me.

I shuddered at the thought and squeezed Hunch tighter in my arms. Despite being on an investigation, he had been struggling to get free, but I wasn't about to let him go. The last thing I needed was to have to go running after him in the backyard of the house I had been directed to stay away from.

"Hi, I'm Mallory," I said in my cheeriest tone. "I just dropped in from out of town to visit my friend across the street . . . " I pointed a thumb over my shoulder, but that second was all I could allow without holding Hunch with two hands. "He doesn't seem to be home, and I wondered if you knew him and happened to know when he might be back?"

My voice had come out casual enough, or at least I'd thought so, but the woman looked at me sidelong, almost ominously. "You say you're a friend?"

"I—uh—an acquaintance, yeah. Why?" My voice had lost its innocence, and now I was fighting with everything in me not to be found out.

"Well, you might want to talk to the local police about your 'acquaintance.'" I could hear the air quotes, even if she didn't use them. "There were two officers by asking about him yesterday, and I'll tell you the same thing I told them." I held my breath, waiting. "I don't know the guy. Never met him. He comes and goes, mostly late at night, and if not for his loud pickup truck, we'd probably never know he was there. Although now that the police are asking after him, you'd better believe I've got my eyes open for the guy."

That must've been why she opened the door so quickly for me. "Is it an old pickup then?"

The woman looked at me sidelong again. "I thought you were his friend."

"Acquaintance," I corrected. "And I haven't seen him in a while." As I said it, I realized I wouldn't be able to ask what this guy looked like, either.

"Yeah, it's an old pickup, light colored, maybe white or beige. If you want to know anything else, I suggest you talk to the police."

With that, she shut the door in my face.

I left her doorstep, stunned at her abruptness, and used all of my strength to keep my wily cat in my arms. I'd only taken a couple of steps away from her house when I saw what had Hunch so riled up.

Amber stood, leaning against the driver's door of my Prius. "Hey," she said, all casual, but I knew her well enough to hear the edge behind her voice.

"Oh. Hey. What are you doing around here?"

She shrugged and pushed off my car. Now that I knew why Hunch was about to claw the blood right out of my arms, I let him jump to the ground, and seconds later, Amber scooped him up. He immediately started purring.

"Well . . . " She drew out the word. "I got permission to drop by your place this afternoon. Seth said he'd drive me on his way to this dinner thing with his girlfriend and pick me up after." She raised her eyebrows, but I waited for more. I was still trying to come up with an excuse I could give her for being in the exact same neighborhood as we'd been in the other night, but at a different house.

Finally, she went on. "So I guess Seth and I were too late because you were already at the stop sign pulling away from your house when we got there. You didn't see us, even though I reached over and honked, and so I told Seth I'd give him ten bucks if he followed you. I figured you were going to the grocery store or something, and I could surprise you there, and we could pick out something to cook. But then I noticed a car was following you, and you were headed farther and farther away from the grocery store.

"When you finally stopped, Seth didn't want to leave me but said he couldn't be late for this thing he was going to with his girlfriend. I wasn't going to leave you out here on your own when it didn't seem like you had any idea that guy was following you. Twenty bucks later, I finally convinced Seth to pull up right behind the car that was following you and rev his engine until the guy left. Seth wanted to know what I was up to, but I only told him I was trying to get your attention. Finally, I spotted you at that house over there, and when I pointed you out, he was willing to leave me."

I blinked a couple of times fast, trying to catch up. "There was a man following me?"

I wondered if that was what had my cat so riled up on the way here or if he'd known Amber was behind us. Either way, I needed to learn to pay more attention to that cat's intuition.

Amber nodded and pulled out her phone. "I took a snapshot of the license plate. I thought you could get Alex to run it, you know, if he's not too busy reading." She still sounded offended.

But I looked closer at the photo, and it was the same dark car, possibly even the same coffee drinker who had been outside my house earlier. Same license plate, too.

So maybe he'd just hidden better.

I got Amber to send me the photo and then took a step toward my driver's door, but Amber stepped into my path.

"Uh-uh," she said. "Not until you tell me what's going on. And this time, save your fake stories. I'm not falling for some fable about you returning a silver platter."

# Chapter Twenty-four

I'D ALWAYS THOUGHT AMBER was too smart for her own good. Now I knew it for sure.

"Look, get in the car and we'll head back to my place. I'll tell you everything there."

She stared at me with serious eyes for a long moment. Finally, she complied. All the way to my house, she stroked Hunch with one hand and tapped her fingers on the armrest with the other, not saying a word. She didn't believe I was going to tell her the truth.

The problem was . . . how could I?

If I got her involved with another investigation, her mom would definitely keep her from seeing me. And as the good role model I was trying to be, the last thing I wanted to do was put Amber in the position where she'd need to lie to her mother.

At the same time, if I let her know I was a possible suspect in an investigation, that could go even worse. Not only could she get grounded from seeing me, but she might also start badgering Alex to the point that the friendship between the three of us completely fell apart.

By the time we got to my house, I took one glance at Amber and knew she was still resolute. I had to say something.

"Do you want coffee?" I asked as I opened my front door.

She let Hunch down and then crossed her arms and raised her eyebrows. "I want answers, Mallory. It's an investigation, isn't it? One you and Alex aren't telling me about?"

As a knee-jerk reaction, I said, "Alex and I are not investigating anything together."

She squinted.

"Just . . . " I grabbed her arm. "Come and sit in the kitchen. I'll tell you everything."

*Everything* wasn't exactly what I told her. I stalled for as long as I could, brewing coffee and warming some frozen baking in the toaster oven. As I worked, I could avoid her eyes and tell her only enough of the story to satisfy her.

Thankfully, once she heard the name Pirro Klytaimnestra, she fixated on him.

"Wait, what? The same guy who impersonated Cooper and tried to make money off his publishing website? And he owns a house now, right here in Honeysuckle Grove?"

Her mentioning Pirro's publishing website reminded me that Alex had been questioning me about Cooper's knowledge of self-publishing. Because this didn't make any immediate sense, I shook it off and told Amber about visiting the title deeds office and how her tip had led me to the Bureau of Corporations and Charitable Organizations website. "From there, I discovered Pirro's name."

"Well, have you told Alex? Is he going to help you take this guy down? Did he send you there to question the neighbors?"

I had to be somewhat honest here, as she'd been spending time with Alex. "Actually, Alex told me to stay away from that neighborhood, so I'd really appreciate it if you wouldn't mention it." I turned from the counter and looked at her with serious eyes. "He doesn't really have time to investigate this with his ridiculously full caseload. I figured if I made sure to stay safe, I could do a little investigating on my own—you know, talking to the neighbors during the day to see what they know and stuff that Alex wouldn't have any time for."

"And returning a silver platter in behind houses late at night?" She gave me a hard stare. I knew it was only out of her concern for my safety, but it suddenly felt as though she were the adult and I were the impetuous teenager.

"Yeah, that was before Alex told me to stay away." I knew she'd have plenty to say about how I'd always warned her to be smart and act cautiously, so I went on before she could lecture me. "I'd only planned to drive by and see if there was a car in the driveway that night, same as today, actually. But once I got there and saw the place deserted, I just had to know more. I mean, this clearly has something to do with me. Why else would this guy be in my hometown?"

"And Alex really isn't doing anything to help?"

I didn't know how to refute this. "He will. I know he will. He's just so busy, but he *is* concerned, and you know what?" I spoke the thought as it came to me. "I wonder if that car that was following me was placed outside my house by him. I'll bet he stationed someone in front of my house, but he didn't want to freak me out, so he didn't say anything."

She nodded slowly. "Okay. So how can I help?"

I shook my head quickly. "You can't. Your mom would freak, and you know you're not allowed to help with investigations. Besides, like I said, I've pretty much done all I can, anyway. I plan to stay far away from that house from now on."

Especially if Alex had had a car trailing me all along. I'd have another fight on my hands when he heard about me going to the neighborhood he'd told me specifically not to.

But that answer wasn't good enough for Amber. "Okay, so what did the neighbor tell you? Had she seen the guy?"

I nodded. "But I'd stupidly gone in pretending to be a friend of Pirro's, so I couldn't exactly ask for a description. She did tell me that he only came and went late at night, though, and he drove a loud pickup truck."

"So probably an older vehicle?" Amber grabbed the notepad from my table and jotted this down. "Did she say what color?"

"Light colored, she said. Beige or white."

Amber nodded, writing. "Doesn't Cooper's old friend that visits you have a light-colored pickup?"

"Pete? Well, yeah, but he lives in Pennsylvania, works there with his dad. Besides, I told him about this whole mess, and he was as freaked out about it as I was. He even went to stake out the house with me one night."

Amber raised an eyebrow. I wasn't sure if it was to make me feel guilty for spending the night in a car with a man or if it was because I'd been investigating without her.

I ignored it. "Besides, why on earth would Pete buy a house under Cooper's name? He loved Cooper and his whole family as much as I did."

Amber looked as though she didn't completely believe this, but she nodded as though she would give me that much for the moment. "But you're not leaving me out of this. I may have to investigate this from my laptop in my bedroom at home, but you'd better believe I'm going to find a way to help."

I believed it. That was what worried me the most.

# Chapter Twenty-five

AMBER AND I MADE a vegan chocolate soufflé to take home to her mom while we discussed every detail I knew about the house on Marsh Avenue and its owner. I'd only ever told Amber snippets about the strange stalker who had set up a private membership-only website under Cooper's name as a moneymaking scheme back when we were first living together, but now I went through the whole story, bit by bit.

After Seth picked her up, I put into motion the only plan Amber and I had come up with.

I dialed Alex.

When he answered in his usual tired tone, I had my prepared script ready. I had decided to pretend our earlier argument hadn't happened, in hopes he would also ignore it for the moment. "Hey, so . . . you know that strange car that was parked on my street?" Before he could answer, I went on. "I led it around town earlier today, just to confirm if it was following me, and it totally was." As I said the words, I realized I probably shouldn't have let a sixteen-year-old write my dialogue for me. "Anyway, I'm back at home now, safe and sound, but I snapped a picture of the license plate. I know you're short on time, but if I send it to you, could you have someone run it to find the owner?"

A long pause followed where all I could hear was Alex's heavy breathing and the quick panting of Hunter in the background. "Okay, look, Mal, I didn't want to say anything because I didn't want to worry you, but I've had an undercover officer watching your house."

Just as Amber and I suspected. "Watching my house or watching me?"

He sighed. "Watching you. But, Mallory, I got word of where you went earlier today and I'm not happy about it."

He was only trying to turn this conversation back on me so I was the one with some explaining to do, but I wasn't done with him yet. "If you have an undercover officer watching me, you either think I'm in danger or you think I might be a danger to someone else."

A pause. "I don't think you're a danger to anyone, Mallory. Except maybe to yourself."

"So you *do* think I'm in danger?" I asked.

"It's just a precaution. But there's more than you know going on. I can tell you that things are looking good as far as clearing your name, though."

This should have been good news, but Alex's serious tone still scared me.

"Can I come by later? I'll tell you what I can then."

There was no way I would refuse him, especially since he was the fountain of knowledge in my very dry desert of confusion. "How does homemade ravioli sound?"

Alex showed up a little after seven. He gave a couple of quick knocks at the front door before heading around back to tie up Hunter. This time, when he squatted to give the dog direction, Hunter looked more intently at Alex and didn't seem nearly as slobbery.

I opened the sliding glass door for him, and he held up his hands toward my cat as soon as he entered. "I know, I know. I smell like dog. Don't worry, I won't come any closer."

Hunch, seemingly understanding this, sniffed the air a couple of times and then went to lie near his food dish. He wasn't

going to hiss at Alex this time, but he also wasn't about to
nuzzle up to him.

Once I had served portions of ravioli, garlic bread, and
Caesar salad for both of us, I sat across from him at my kitchen
table. He took three big bites, barely chewed, and swallowed
before filling me in.

"I'm going to keep a car outside for now, but the officer
knows that you know about him, and if you have any concerns,
feel free to go outside and talk to him yourself. His name's
Jim."

I nodded, picking at my bread. I'd yet to take a bite. "But you
do think I'm in danger?"

"Not necessarily *danger*. But I'm concerned about some of
the people Cooper associated with."

"Don't you think it would be in my best interest to know
what's going on?"

He took in a breath and let it out in a sigh. "I suppose." He
looked at me. "We have reason to believe that Ron Beckford
had some business dealings that involved Cooper—or possibly someone posing as Cooper—right here in Honeysuckle
Grove. I spoke with a couple of people at the bank after I
questioned you the other day, and they were able to confirm
someone was posing as you to access an account there. Steve
and I agree that you're no longer a serious suspect in our case,
but he still doesn't want me sharing the case details with you."

I opened my mouth but closed it when nothing came out. I
opened my mouth again to ask if Ron Beckford had been seen
in town and if I should be worried about leaving my house, but
Alex cut me off before I could.

"Now, I understand you visited a house on Marsh Avenue
today. I need you to tell me everything Mrs. Rainer told you."

Mrs. Rainer must have been the neighbor I'd spoken to.
"She really didn't tell me anything. She said the police had

already been around asking about the owner of the house across the street."

"You didn't go in posing as police?" He raised an eyebrow at me.

"No, I wasn't about to do that when you expressly told me to keep out of it." I offered a wry smile and took a bite, chewing and making him wait for answers for once. "She only said that the guy only ever came and went late at night and that he drove a loud pickup truck."

"A light-colored pickup truck," Alex added, looking at his notes from the chair beside him. "Doesn't your friend Pete also drive a light-colored pickup?"

I sighed, annoyed that this was the second time today I'd had to defend Pete. "Yes, but believe me, Pete has nothing to do with this. When you were too busy and I couldn't get a hold of you . . . back when I was under investigation," I added, "Pete actually went over there to stake out the house with me. He's worried for my safety, too, and he was pretty freaked out when I told him the guy who had stalked Cooper had set up a corporation under Cooper's name right here in town."

"He was?" I couldn't tell by his tone if Alex believed this. "So you spent the whole night alone in a car with this Pete Kline?"

I gritted my teeth. He was judging me again, and the only reason I was even with Pete at all was because Alex wasn't around. "We're only good friends. Honestly, it was a really healing night for both of us, telling stories and remembering Cooper together."

Alex nodded. "What does Pete do for work? Did you say he went to college with Cooper? Was he in the writing program?"

"He was," I hedged, drawing out the words. I didn't know if Alex was asking out of interest or if he was in investigative mode. "But he had to give that up in his last year before getting his master's. His dad made him quit to work with his construction company. I think he's been picking up the writing a little again lately, which makes me so happy. Cooper always used to say a writer isn't complete unless he's writing."

Alex took a few more quick bites of his ravioli, finishing his plate while I was lost in thoughts about Cooper and his pithy sayings.

"Oh. Can I get you more?" I asked, but Alex was already headed to the sink with his plate. He rinsed it and put it into the dishwasher.

"No, I should really go. But, Mallory, can I ask you something?" He turned and looked at me with serious eyes.

I stood, even though my plate was still mostly full. "Okay," I told him cautiously.

And I was good to be cautious because he then told me, "Stay away from Pete Kline *and* that house on Marsh Avenue—just until I can prove they're unrelated."

My hands flew up at my sides. "First you're accusing Cooper and then me, and now you're accusing Pete? For all this work you and Steve are doing, you're looking in the complete wrong direction!"

At my distress, Alex backed toward the sliding glass door, eager to get out of here.

But I had more to say. "I'm sick and tired of you questioning my judgment and absolutely everyone I've ever trusted! Maybe it's time you looked at yourself and why you feel the need to condemn every person I've ever known."

He opened his mouth but then closed it again, and his jaw tightened. Only a second later, he turned and left without another word.

I was glad Alex was taking the house on Marsh Avenue seriously. Soon he'd figure out that Ron Beckford might be someone to worry about, but Pete Kline was not. He'd been the saving grace for Cooper's entire family and, at least to some degree, for me.

As soon as Alex disappeared from my backyard, I slumped into my chair and let out a heavy sigh. But could I trust my own judgment? More than once, I'd questioned if Cooper may have been keeping big secrets from me. And what if Alex was right about there being connections I couldn't see?

I tried to figure out what my instincts were telling me, but I didn't know anymore. I had no idea what to believe or who to trust.

# Chapter Twenty-six

As THE NEXT DAY passed, I became more and more frustrated with Alex's cryptic answers. I'd been honest and upfront with him, and yet he kept holding back information and then getting upset with me when I tried to find it on my own. My patience had run out. His excuse that he couldn't share information with me because I was involved was sounding less and less believable. If the case clearly involved me, shouldn't he be upfront with everything he knew?

I was also becoming increasingly bothered by Pete's truck being similar to the one at the house on Marsh Avenue. Not at all because I thought Pete could own the house, but because Alex, and even Amber, felt they had some legitimate reason for me to stay away from my old friend—the only one I could share memories of Cooper with and the only person I could talk honestly with at all these days. I was tired of being alone.

I spent the rest of the afternoon making a therapy list for Dr. Harrison, listing my arguments with Alex, him secretly posting an officer outside of my house, and his and Amber's suspicion of Pete and his truck. There was still so much disconnect between Pirro, Ron, and Cooper, along with the house on Marsh Avenue because that was where all this activity was centered. But list making wasn't helping. If anything, it was making me realize just how strange this situation was and that I was missing vital information to help figure out how these details fit together.

I knew I shouldn't do it, and yet, late that night, when I couldn't sleep, I decided to take a quick drive-by of the house and hopefully the owner's truck. I could snap a quick photo of the license plate and prove once and for all that Pete was not involved in whatever scam Alex was investigating.

I brought Hunch, of course.

And I convinced myself that this was okay because Alex clearly didn't have time to do it himself.

But maybe I was wrong because the moment I turned the corner onto Marsh Avenue, lights shone out through the front windows of the house in question, and Alex's unmarked police car—on which I'd long ago memorized the license plate numbers—sat squarely in its driveway.

I squinted at the dark street in front of me and, about ten houses down, spotted an old white pickup truck. I idled in place, surveying the situation. Hunch was on alert in the passenger seat and let out a low growl when I hesitated.

"But if I drive by and Alex sees me," I told my cat, "isn't that only going to make me look guiltier in the case he'd just pretty much cleared me from?"

Hunch kept his eyes trained on the suspicious house. He ignored my concerns and growled deeper.

"How about this?" I asked, as though I needed my cat's permission. "I'll drive around the block and come at it from the other side. We can have a closer look at that truck. I mean, that's what we really came here for anyway, right?"

At least Hunch stopped his growling as soon as I was moving again.

The suburban neighborhood was not as easy to navigate as I'd hoped. It took me three tries at either dead-end streets or ones that ended up winding in different directions to finally find the other end of Marsh Avenue. I turned onto it and crept along until I came to the old, white pickup. Now that I could see it more closely, it also had a few big rust patches and a thin blue stripe along the side.

Just like Pete's.

I refrained from taking a photo and instead moved forward so I could see the license plate, as it didn't have one on the front. I gasped the second it came into view and pulled my camera phone down to my lap quickly.

It *was* Pete's truck!

My eyes darted toward Alex's unmarked police car and the house in front of it. There was no movement from within that I could see. My mind whirred.

Why would Pete purchase a house under Cooper's name, and was he truly posing as Pirro? If Pete was involved with this Cooper Beck LLC house, Alex clearly knew enough to come here and confront him, and maybe he had good reason to ask me to steer clear of Pete until he could figure it out. But this must be based on more than just a similarly colored truck. I picked up my phone again and hesitated, then clicked to Alex's contact and hit DIAL. It was time for Alex to tell me what he knew.

But his phone rang and rang until his voice mail picked up. I hesitated, then let out a stream of confusion and anger. "Look, I know you're at the Marsh Avenue house and you clearly have more information about Pete than you let on. If you'd just be honest with me, Alex—" My voice broke so I stopped talking.

I didn't know how to finish that sentence anyway. If he'd just be honest with me then . . . what? I wouldn't feel like I was crazy? I wouldn't feel like there was no one in the world I could trust? I still couldn't believe that Pete had been lying to me about the house while staking it out with me. There had to be another explanation.

"Just . . . call me back," I said into my phone, and then I hung up.

I couldn't just go home. I couldn't.

Even though I'd promised not to, I scrolled until I found Pete's number, but the same thing happened. No answer, and this time, I had no words when his voice mail picked up.

I drove slowly past the house, hoping Alex *would* see me. It would give me a reason to confront both of them for some answers. But even though there were lights on near the front of the house, the curtains were closed and I couldn't see anyone.

Hunch's growls became louder, and he pawed at the passenger side window, trying to get out.

"If only I had your courage," I told my cat. "I'd just walk up to the front door, bang on it, and demand some answers." As I said the words, a small bit of peace came over me.

Because why couldn't I do that? Sure, it might make me look guiltier in some respects, but I hadn't done anything illegal, at least not knowingly. These two men were both my good friends. I was tired—exhausted, really—from all the secrets and lies. I needed to have everything out in the open once and for all, regardless of the fallout. I didn't believe either of them were out to hurt me or send me to prison, even if I could be tied to some sort of crime. I should have nothing to worry about.

Still, I pulled up a good ten car lengths away from the house and then parked along the curb, like I might be able to make a quick getaway if I needed to.

As soon as my car was in park, Hunch let out a loud meow, as if I might have forgotten he was there and left him behind.

"Oh, don't worry. You're coming, buddy," I told him. "You're about the only one in this situation I feel like I can trust."

I held my door open so he could hop out after me. I decided against scooping him up into my arms. Once Alex or Pete answered the door, I had no doubt Hunch, if left to his own devices, would dart inside to come up with his own intel.

He didn't wait for me and trotted back down the road toward the house.

"Hey, wait for me," I whisper-hissed. But he paid me no attention so I picked up to a quiet jog.

By the time I got to the front walkway, I didn't see Hunch anywhere, but as I neared Alex's car, barking erupted from inside.

"It's only me, Hunter," I whispered, but that didn't calm him down any. The house didn't show any movement, so if Alex was inside, he must not be able to hear his dog.

"Hunch?" I whispered over Hunter's barking. "Where are you?"

I couldn't explain it, but I felt much more vulnerable and even less capable without my ten-pound tabby.

Movement flickered out of the corner of my eye from around the side of the house. That was where I'd gone the other night and left my silver platter. Hunch had seen me go that direction, so it made sense he thought I'd go that way again.

I tiptoed across the grass toward the path at the side of the house, and sure enough, I caught sight of him sniffing the silver platter that still rested near the back corner of the house, moonlight glinting off it.

"Hunch!" I whispered again. "Come back here! We're going to the front door." As I said the words, I envisioned how crazy Hunter would go with Hunch padding near his owner's car.

Hunch paid me no attention, anyway, and instead wandered around the back of the house.

I sighed inwardly and followed. Part of me was probably stalling on confronting Alex and Pete, but I also really needed Hunch with me.

I finally caught up to him near the rear glass door. I hesitated as two figures inside came into view. Even from their backs, I could tell it was Alex and Pete, but they were headed toward the front of the house. Alex wore his detective suit, while Pete wore heather-gray sweatpants and a white T-shirt.

I waited in the shadows until they disappeared from the dining room area. That was when I noticed the books that were laid out beside the laptop on the table. They had been rearranged so I could see one of the covers, and it was the same Peter Becker novel I'd just read the other night, called *Vain Glory*.

As the title came into view, the name Peter Becker suddenly struck me. Were those *Pete's* books? Had he set up a writing haven in town here to try and make himself a success using Cooper's name as his home base? I knew I was reaching for explanations and I could be way off, but something about this felt like it could be true.

But then who was Pirro Klytaimnestra?

It was a Greek name. Pete's family was Greek. Had they changed their names at some point?

I could get my head around Pete wanting to use Cooper's name as an homage, and also to hide behind so his dad never found out about his writing pursuits, but I couldn't put together what it would mean if Pete and Pirro were the same person. Did that mean Pete had been Cooper's stalker all those years ago? Or did he only copy the impersonator's name? But then that begged the question of why? And why would Pete lie to me about owning this house and then stake it out with me overnight? Did he not feel like he could be honest with me either?

But then I reminded myself of what a good friend Pete had been to me for years and how he'd supported Cooper's family during their grief. No, if Pete had tried to use anyone's name, I had to believe it was only to honor Cooper's memory.

When I was certain Pete and Alex were out of eyeshot, I moved closer, took a photo of the stack of books with my phone, and then quickly reached to grab Hunch from where he sniffed at the glass door.

"Nope, we're going to hurry around to the front yard," I whispered to him. "That's where we'll find the people who can give us some answers."

# Chapter Twenty-seven

"AND WHAT'S THE NAME of your father's construction company?" Alex asked loudly enough that I could hear as I made it to the Marsh Avenue house's front corner. I stayed hidden around the side of the house, out of view but within earshot.

As Pete told him, my phone buzzed from my pocket. I snatched it up, hoping they wouldn't hear the buzz. Then a second later, I wondered if it could somehow be Alex or Pete getting back to me in the midst of their conversation.

I shook my head at myself when I saw it was only a text from Amber.

**~Found out something interesting about that book Alex wanted. It might be linked to the house over on Marsh Ave. Call me!!!~**

"What are your hours with Kline Construction?" Alex asked. "And what exactly do you do?"

Pete went into a long description of the variety of duties he performed for his dad's company. I knew from many conversations with Pete, not to mention the amount he'd helped even me and Cooper repair items around our house, that he was a jack of all trades and this description could take a while.

As much as I was determined not to get Amber involved, being out here on my own with so many questions, I felt the need to have one person I could trust at least know where I was. I turned my phone to silent so it wouldn't buzz again and texted her back.

**~I'm there now. Alex is questioning Pete about his job.
I think he might be the author of those books!~**

**~And the owner of that house!~** Amber shot back.

All evidence did point to that, but then I kept coming back
to the question of why Pete would have sat outside all night
with me, pretending he knew nothing about it. If he had told
me it was his writing haven and he'd bought the house in
Cooper's name to honor him, I would have had nothing but
respect for that.

Then Alex regained my attention. "And you have no knowledge of a man named Pirro Klytaimnestra who owns this
house?"

"I do not, but you'd better believe I'll let you know the
second I find this Pirro character." Pete sounded righteously
angry. I tilted my head, trying to understand. Did that mean
Pete wasn't Pirro? If he wasn't, why was he here? "But, listen,"
he went on. "When you contact my dad, ask him all you want
about my work hours, but would you mind not mentioning the
book stuff? He doesn't have much tolerance for that sort of
thing."

"You've been writing and publishing behind your father's
back?" Alex asked the same thing I was wondering. But this
part quickly made sense because Mr. Kline really was a bear
when it came to his son's creative pursuits. After all, he'd made
his son drop out of college only a year away from getting his
master's degree. "For the time being, I see no reason to inform
him of your publishing pursuits. And you said you are the sole
electrician for Kline Construction. Is that right?" Alex asked.

"Electricians come and go. It's that type of trade. But right
now the only one, yeah. That's why Dad freaks out if I head
out of town for more than a couple of days."

I didn't know all of that, but it made sense with what I knew
of Pete's dad. Still, I wasn't sure why Alex was dwelling on

Pete's work schedule. It seemed as though he had as much as admitted he was the author of the Peter Becker novels, and he was only here to try and catch Pirro Klytaimnestra, so those bits of information seemed unconnected.

But then it hit me.

Pete was Kline Construction's only electrician. He had written a novel under a pseudonym that practically outlined how Cooper's death had occurred. Why would he have included such detail in that part, except perhaps for therapeutic reasons, the same way I'd been writing my lists for Dr. Harrison?

But I got the feeling Alex didn't have the same understanding. Was he investigating Pete and his books because he thought they were somehow connected to Cooper's death?

Once again, the part of me that had never believed Cooper's death had been an accident rose up within me and quickened my breath.

I had to know the truth.

And I had to find it out tonight.

# Chapter Twenty-eight

I HAD ALMOST WORKED up my courage to confront them both when Alex asked Pete, "So you'll be in town until Monday?"

"Yes, Monday morning," Pete said. His answer made me remember how Donna Mayberry had thought she'd seen Pete around town more than once. It seemed she hadn't been mistaken.

"Please let me know if you need to leave town any time before then. I realize you have to return to Pennsylvania to your job, but until we've solved this case, I need to be able to reach you. Is this the best number?" He rattled off Pete's cell number, which I knew by heart.

"Absolutely," Pete told him, nothing but helpful. I was glad to finally have Alex and Pete aligned on the same team, even if they were both holding back a lot of information from me. "I'll keep my phone on, and I'll let you know if this Pirro guy shows up at the house."

A second later, Alex's footsteps sounded down the front cement path. He didn't ask all of the many questions I was dying to ask, but one thing was sure. It seemed I'd get more answers out of Pete than I would out of Alex.

Pete, who was finally publishing his books but had to keep them a secret from his dad. Pete, who was secretly staking out the house in Cooper's name because he was just as worried about this Pirro guy as I was.

Meanwhile, Alex was so stuck on the idea of keeping me away from the situation, perhaps he wasn't thinking clearly.

I waited until Alex's car disappeared down the street, took a deep breath, and then headed for the front door. Hunch wanted down from my arms, and I had no problem with that. Now that I had a better handle on how Pete was involved, Hunch could do what he pleased while I asked a few pointed questions.

I waited a good couple of minutes to make sure Alex was really gone and then headed up the front steps. It was after eleven at night, so it surprised me when the door swung open after I'd barely knocked on it. Pete stood on the other side, clearly expecting it to be Alex again. I recognized his smile—the same false smile he'd worn for professors back in college when he was trying to get extensions on projects.

His smile flattened when he saw me. Then his gaze darted behind me to the street in either direction and back to my face before he finally said, "Mallory?"

"Yes, Mallory." Hunch had already darted inside between Pete's legs, so I took a note from my cat and pushed past him to get through the door. "What's going on? Why are you here?"

I knew the reason. He was staking out the place until Pirro Klytaimnestra came back, but I wanted to start with a bit of truth and work from there toward the rest of the things he hadn't told me.

As I moved out of the entryway and into the unfurnished living room, I almost tripped on a duffel bag that was filled with clothes and the laptop I'd seen in the dining room a few minutes ago. The books were stuffed on top so the zipper couldn't close.

"I was worried about this Pirro guy." Pete swallowed a couple of times between sentences, telling me he was flustered by my sudden appearance. "It really freaked me out when you said it was the same guy who had been impersonating Cooper all those years ago, and now he's living in your hometown? I'm doing this to protect you, Mallory. I broke in, and I was hoping if I stayed here long enough, I'd catch him coming back to this place and find out what he's all about." Pete caught his breath and looked at me with serious eyes. "Now that Cooper's gone, someone has to look after you."

I glanced at the duffel bag again. "But now you're leaving? And didn't you just tell Alex you'd be here until Monday?"

I snapped my mouth shut. I hadn't wanted to let on that I'd been eavesdropping, but I was tired, and I so desperately wanted the truth.

Pete shook his head and then looked at me for several long seconds before answering. "Oh, I wasn't leaving. I'm here until Monday, just like I told Detective Martinez."

I didn't think I was imagining the sudden clip to his voice when he said Alex's title. But I kept looking between him and his duffel bag.

He shook his head again, as if answering my inner questions. "I pack up each night and head down to the basement. Apparently, this Pirro guy only ever shows up really late into the night, so I clear all my stuff out and hide. One of these nights, I'm going to catch him."

So the neighbor, Mrs. Rainer, must have been confused and thought Pete was the one living here when she saw his truck. But more importantly, was Pete really that concerned for me that he'd driven all the way from Pennsylvania the moment he had a couple of days off to try and catch this guy?

"What about your private investigator? Did he find something out about this guy?" The situation had to be more dangerous than I knew.

Pete rubbed the back of his neck and stared at the floor. Pink crept up his cheeks. "Well, I kind of lied about that. I don't have a private investigator friend. I've been trying to find out what I can on my own. But, Mal, you should get out of here quickly before the guy shows up."

How did he know exactly when this Pirro guy might show up? My stomach got that queasy feeling that I'd been getting every time I found out something new about this investigation, but I crossed my arms to hide it. If Pete had been deceiving me, too, who could I trust? Alex was completely closed off. Amber, while willing to help, didn't know the full scope of what was going on. I wasn't done asking questions. At least Pete might be willing to be honest with me and tell me everything he knew if I drew it out of him.

"If you're staking out the place, I'll do it with you." I stared at him, resolute.

And he must have seen the determination in my eyes because he took in a deep breath, let it out, and then led me down the hallway and around a corner to open a door to what must have been the basement. He looked like he was going to follow me, empty-handed.

"Don't you need to grab your stuff, too?" I reminded him. I wanted him to see the novels at the top of his duffel bag and explain those without having to ask, but at the same time, I understood. If he felt the need to keep his creative ventures secret from his dad, he probably just got in a habit of keeping them quiet from everyone.

He nodded. "I'll be down in a sec. I have to find that cat of yours or he'll be a dead giveaway that someone's been in here." His voice sounded off, but I figured he was only trying to hurry me along. He flicked on a light switch in the stairwell, but it didn't do anything. "Oh, there's another switch at the bottom. That one works."

I was a few steps down when I realized that even though I may not have much success corralling Hunch, Pete, who didn't even like cats, would have even less. I turned back to say, "I should probably get Hunch," but Pete had already let the door close behind me, leaving me in the dark.

"It's no problem. I'll find him," he said through the door. But I had to at least help.

I reached for the doorknob and tried to turn it, but it had no give. "Hey, this door must lock from the other side. Hey, Pete?"

His footsteps moved around loudly on the other side of the door, but he didn't say anything for a long minute. The silence, along with the reminder of all the horror movies I'd watched lately, started to bottom out my stomach. I tried the door again. Still locked.

"Hey, Pete. Unlock the door. This isn't funny."

Finally, Pete spoke, but his voice didn't bring the relief I was looking for. "Your new boyfriend just had to keep asking questions, didn't he? I can't believe you think it's okay to jump into some kind of heavy romance when Coop's barely in the grave. Are you sleeping with him?" I felt so momentarily flustered by the accusation, I almost missed his next question. "Is that how you got him to look into Cooper's death?"

*Cooper's death?* Pete's tone didn't just make my stomach drop, it made it completely hollow out when I realized what was happening here.

"Why did you do it, Pete?" My voice was a ragged whisper. "Just tell me that."

Pete must have heard me. "I'd only planned to take the guy down a notch. He had everything and I had nothing, and he didn't even seem to care about every bit of good fortune that came his way. We had a great opportunity with his Uncle Ron, creating a self-publishing company and sinking enough money into each book that they would become instant best-sellers, but he was too stupid to take it. So I took the opportunity without him. I started a corporation under Coop's name. Beckford never knew the difference and thought he was laundering all his money directly through his nephew.

"Except when Coop started to ask questions, and I tried to tell him everything, he freaked out and told me he was going to the bank to intercept Ron as he made a cash deposit and tell him we wanted no part of it anymore. I tried to call Ron, to warn him and let him know what had happened, but he said if I didn't fix it, it would be my head on the chopping block. I thought a near-death experience was what Coop needed to put things into perspective and realize that neither of us wanted to cross Ron Beckford."

"Near death?" I whispered. I dropped down onto a stair and put my head between my knees. I couldn't believe what I was hearing.

"The guy should have had plenty of time to get out." Pete's voice sounded like a pained cry. "I still don't know why he didn't or why he ended up near the rear break room of the bank."

I could picture exactly what had happened, had envisioned it many times. Someone from the back of the bank had called out for help. Probably one of the two other people who had died along with Cooper that day. He'd spent so much time writing about his hero, Marty Sims, and he always said he wanted to do something heroic like Marty one day.

I let out a humorless laugh, feeling emptier than I ever had in my life. I asked the question that still burned inside of me. "So you didn't have any concern that everyone might not get out of the bank alive?"

But I was only greeted with silence. And then I heard the front door close.

# Chapter Twenty-nine

I BANGED ON THE door. I rammed it with my shoulder, which only knocked me down a few darkened stairs and twisted my ankle.

And then I smelled smoke.

Only a second later, a loud beeping smoke alarm on the other side of the door went off.

Was this possible? Could Pete have really been so concerned at burying his secrets that he'd started a fire and left me to die? He would kill me to protect himself?

As smoke crept under the door where a small sliver of light came through, I pulled off my sweater and pushed it into the gap. I limped as quickly as I could down the stairs and pawed every wall within reach, but I found no light switches at all in the cement basement. Why should I be surprised that he'd been lying about that, too? I turned in every direction, looking for the glow of streetlights through a window, but there didn't seem to be any windows.

Pete had once told me that some landowners paid his dad a lot of money under the table to build houses with secret basements that weren't filed in the plans. Apparently, this was usually to run underground drug growing operations. This house looked like it may have been built for that purpose, but not yet used.

I remembered my phone in my back pocket and pulled it out, but surrounded by cement on all sides, it had no bars.

I used the flashlight to look around the basement and, in a second, could tell Pete had been lying about ever spending time down here. The room was completely bare, with cement floors and unfinished two-by-four framing. I tried to take my phone back up the stairs, but it was getting so smoky, I could barely make out the screen. I fumbled over it, trying to get the phone app open to dial 911, but in the process, I accidentally dialed Amber's number since she had been my last contact.

She picked up before I realized I'd dialed her. "Oh, good, it's you! Wait'll you hear—"

"Amber! Call 911! Pete locked me in the basement of the Marsh house and started a fire!" That was all I could get out before I started hacking and had to race to the bottom of the stairs to catch my breath. I pulled the phone to my ear again and called out to Amber, but I'd lost reception.

Then scratching sounded at the top door. It only took me a second to recognize it. "Hunch! Get outside, Hunchie! Go get help! You have to get out of the smoke!"

I hacked out another cough, but the frantic scratching continued. I turned on my phone's flashlight and scanned the basement once more. The only thing my flashlight revealed was smoke.

Lots and lots of smoke.

I dropped to the floor where the air was clearest and took shallow breaths, trying to think. And then I prayed.

Because if anyone could get me out of this, God could.

# Chapter Thirty

WHEN I HEARD THE first siren, I was face-first on the cement with my shirt over my mouth and nose, nearly passed out from coughing. As the fireman carried me out, I squeezed my eyes shut against the thick smoke and was nearly blindsided by moonlight and streetlights when he finally reached the outside, oxygenated world. He laid me down on the grass, took my pulse, and shone a flashlight into my pupils.

Several other firemen hosed down the smoking house, but it seemed like they'd already extinguished any large flames. Yellow-striped barricades had been placed at the edge of the property near the road, but Amber dodged them, paying little attention to the rules as she and a woman I didn't recognize raced toward me.

"Are you okay?" Amber asked, frantic.

The woman with her asked, "Do you want some water?" and then called out, "Somebody get Mallory some water!"

That was when I recognized Helen Montrose, with her usual auburn bouffant hairstyle flat against her head and wearing a beige sweatsuit, which, in any other circumstance, I never would have been able to picture on her.

"I'm fine," I rasped out, but hearing my own voice, I likely did need some water. I hadn't realized until this moment how much smoke I'd likely inhaled.

Once the fireman decided I'd be fine under mother-and-daughter Montrose care, he left to check on the remnants of the fire. Helen marched off to track down a glass of water from one of the neighbors who looked on from the street.

"What are you doing here?" I asked Amber. My throat felt a little less raspy the more I used it.

Amber shook her head. "I didn't know the address on Marsh Avenue. I called 911, but I was afraid they wouldn't know which house, and since our place is so close, I told Mom you were in danger and we had to come and help. Of course, I wasn't counting on the fact that there'd be flames shooting out of every window, so it was pretty obvious which house by the time I got here."

My eyes widened. "Really?"

Amber nodded and then motioned to the front porch. "If not for Hunch, they may not have gotten to you in time. There was a lot of smoke, and it was hard enough for them to get inside without the place collapsing, but Hunch knew exactly where the basement door was and led the way like a soldier. Apparently, he'd scratched it up something awful trying to get to you."

I looked toward where Hunch sat on his haunches near the front door of the smoking house, as if he was directing the fire dousing operation. My heart had been warming toward that cat, but it was incomparable to what I felt for him right that second. "Where's Alex? Does he know what happened?"

Amber held up her phone. "I've been texting him updates to let him know what was happening with you. He was already out of town and had an idea of which way Pete was headed. He didn't want to miss his chance to catch him."

"And did he?" I still couldn't believe Pete had been willing to leave me there to die. He had actually meant to *kill* me. And had he truly been responsible for killing Cooper?

"Not yet," she said. "But hopefully soon."

Yes, hopefully soon. Because I needed some closure for this. Some irrefutable answers.

# Chapter Thirty-one

THE FIREMEN CALLED FOR an ambulance for me, even though I said I felt fine, and sent me to the hospital. The last thing I saw as two paramedics closed the doors on the back of the ambulance was Amber, holding a very tired Hunch in her arms, with her mother's arm around her.

Her mother, despite her strong allergy to all animals with fur, wasn't letting Hunch keep her away from her daughter. Helen Montrose wiped her runny nose and looked as though the whole crazy incident had infused her with a little perspective on her life and how much she needed to be present for her daughter.

Gazing at the three of them, I figured maybe something good had come out of all of this, anyway.

It was sometime in the middle of the night, when I was trying in vain to sleep in a hospital bed, that I finally heard from Alex.

He peeked through my hospital room door to check on me, probably assuming I would be sleeping.

"Did you catch him?" I asked. My throat was still raw from the smoke. The doctor said it would take a few days to heal.

Alex stood in the doorway for several long seconds, as if debating whether to walk away or come inside.

"Oh, come on," I said, pushing myself up to a seated position. "After everything that's happened, you can't really be ready to walk away and keep more secrets from me?"

He pushed through my door and came inside, and for the
first time, I saw the bags under his eyes, the utter exhaustion.
"No, no. It's not that. I just didn't want to keep you awake.
The nurse was pretty rude out there." He motioned over his
shoulder. "Gave me a good talking to about interrupting you
when you need your rest."

I let out a humorless laugh. "I don't even need to be in
here." My scratchy voice betrayed this sentiment, but I went
on anyway. "Ironically, they kept me so I could rest up and
heal, but I'd have a much better chance of getting a good
night's sleep at home."

I wasn't completely sure if that were true. After all, without
knowing where Pete was or if he'd been caught, I likely would
have been tossing and turning in my own bed just as much.

"Anyway, I caught him," Alex said, rubbing the back of his
neck. "Or, rather, Hunter did."

"Really?" My eyes widened. "How? Where?"

"In my research, I'd found out that Ron Beckford kept a boat
moored at Colonial Beach." Colonial Beach was the nearest
beach to Honeysuckle Grove, about a forty-five-minute drive
away. "Pete was writing novels under a pen name, and in two
out of the three of them, the main character escaped the
shady police force by boat."

I remembered that! I wouldn't have taken notice of that co-
incidence and once again was enlightened on Alex's brilliance
as a detective.

"I hadn't trusted Pete one bit when I interviewed him earlier tonight, but I also hadn't thought of him as an immediate
threat to anyone." Alex looked at me with a serious gaze. I
knew what that gaze meant. Pete *wouldn't* have been a danger
if I hadn't been snooping around for my own answers. I had a
thing or two to say about that, but for the moment, I wanted to
hear the rest of Alex's story. "I was headed back to the office

to research everything Pete had told me about his father's company and the electrical wiring from the bank."

"Did he kill Cooper?" I blurted the question, interrupting Alex, because I had to hear it again, this time from Alex. It seemed too hard to believe that Pete could have done something so horrible and then been acting magnanimous and helpful to both me and Cooper's family for over a year.

Alex looked down at his shoes, which told me everything I needed to know. When he returned my gaze again, he nodded solemnly. "We think so. There was another fire at the downtown post office this past November. It was being debated whether or not to label it as arson, and when discussing it with the forensics team, they mentioned that arson could be difficult to prove when the cause seemed to be old electrical wiring. Because no one was injured, they wanted to call it out as a public case of arson. That made me think of what had happened to Cooper, and I went digging around. That, too, had a note about suspected arson, but it was never publicized because it couldn't be proven one way or the other and I suspect Corbett didn't want the families of the deceased fighting for justice where he likely wouldn't be able to give them any justice."

I stared at my lap, trying to take this all in. "So you've suspected this since November."

He let out a heavy breath. "I had nothing to go on but a gut feeling until just recently. Until I read the third novel in Peter Becker's new series, actually."

I shook my head, pained all over again. "Was Pete truly *bragging* about killing his best friend?"

I just couldn't believe that. He might have had more going on inside of him than I realized, but I couldn't believe he was pure evil.

"I suspect it had more to do with purging his guilt than bragging. From what he revealed when I interviewed him, I don't know that the guy has had anyone he could be honest with through his entire life. He's going to go to prison for a long time, but he also needs a good round of therapy."

"Don't we all?"

"I'll know more after I have a talk with him tomorrow. Hopefully, after a few hours of rest." He glanced at the time on his phone. It was after three.

This was my cue to tell him to go and sleep, I knew that. But I had more to get off my chest, and I feared I wouldn't bring myself to do it during the light of day.

"Look, I understand why you didn't tell me about your suspicions of Cooper's death right away, but there's a lot you weren't trusting me with, Alex."

He shook his head and rubbed his neck. "I was only trying to protect you."

"Protecting someone doesn't mean shutting them out and treating them as though they don't matter."

He looked at me, stunned for a second, as if he'd never considered that this was how I might have felt. He picked up my hand and held it. "I never meant . . . "

I tried to explain. "All my questions and confusion, it led me not to trust my own judgment. I never would have walked into such a dangerous situation with Pete, but I didn't feel like I had anyone to talk to or anyone who would be honest with me."

Alex furrowed his brow as he looked at the floor and took this in. Then he nodded. "You're right. I made some bad choices. But please know it was only based on wanting to keep you safe. I used Steve's authority as an excuse, but it was never about him. I just didn't want you hurt. But I see now how I was acting overprotective and how you deserved to know the truth about this, even if I didn't know all of it myself."

"Well. Maybe I gave you some reason for being overprotective," I had to admit. "It was hard to trust you when I couldn't even seem to trust myself and my own intuition."

Finally, he met my gaze. "I promise to do better in the future. If you're still willing to keep me around?"

In that one promise, I knew I hadn't lost complete faith in Alex as a friend or even my trust in myself. Neither of us had made good decisions, but we could do better next time.

We *would* do better next time.

# Chapter Thirty-two

DESPITE HUNCH'S LOUD AND growly objections, Amber and I spent the afternoon baking up dog biscuits the next Saturday. Hunter deserved a reward for chasing down Pete at the docks and getting a good grip on his pant leg to slow him down.

Apparently, through all of his training, Hunter hadn't learned much about keeping quiet and calm, but he had learned how to track a scent. Alex had asked for a copy of one of Peter Becker's books, just playing it off as being a fan of the thriller genre. The book had given Hunter Pete's scent. The moment he got word about the fire on Marsh Avenue, Alex had known Pete had left town. Of course he hadn't realized I was trapped in the basement until he was well out of town toward Colonial Beach.

With Alex coming over today to brief us, I wasn't stupid enough to think I could let Hunter into the house to swoon over him with thanks. But it was a beautiful sunny day, so I'd set up my patio furniture in my backyard, and along with the dog biscuits, we'd made fried chicken, a sour-cream-filled baked potato salad, and we had the crepe batter ready to make some fresh dessert crepes when the time came.

"Should I put the food outside?" Amber asked once the potato salad was in a serving bowl.

Ever since last week on Marsh Avenue, Amber and her mother had been more open with one another than they'd ever been. Amber was allowed to spend time with me again, as long as she was honest about where she was going and what we'd be doing, and they'd even started to talk about their grief over Amber's dad with each other.

"With a puppy outside, I'm thinking we should serve up our plates inside."

She laughed. "Right-o. You'd never try to steal the food off our table, would you, Hunchie?"

Hunch wound his way around Amber's ankles, purring his agreement. She was talking to him constantly and lapping up his friendliness before the enemy arrived. I'd already made up a special tuna surprise for Hunch the morning I'd gotten home from the hospital. He'd helped the firemen find me, after all. If he would have appreciated it, I'd have given him a Medal of Honor for it.

Alex knocked on the glass door right then. I'd gotten used to him coming around back when he had Hunter with him, as well as Hunch hissing and skirting off to the other end of the house. Today, Hunch hissed, but he hopped up onto the small stepladder I kept near my pantry and, from there, to the top of the fridge. His fur poked out straight on all sides, but he could see the backyard from his vantage point, so this still seemed like progress.

Alex and I had spoken by phone several times throughout the week. He had told me bits and pieces of what he'd uncovered while taking Pete's statement, but because of Pete's erratic emotional state, he thought it would be better to discuss the whole story when we could meet up in person.

Once we had our food served and were seated outside, trying to keep our plates from a very eager puppy, Amber was the one to get us started. "Pete was always jealous of Cooper's writing success, so that was his motive?"

Alex shook his head as he finished a bite of chicken. "Not just his writing success, but his family, too. And his wife." Alex glanced at me. "He had convinced himself that he could be just as good of a son, brother, and spouse to all of them as Cooper had been, and working hard at that kept him from looking at what he had done."

Amber didn't feel the need to leave a beat of time for me to take this in. "And Ron Beckford offered to publish Pete's books so he could launder his money through Pete's publishing company?"

"Not exactly." Alex took another bite. I liked seeing him more relaxed, and I knew I'd get all of my answers today before he left, which made me relax, too. He'd make sure of it. "Ron was only willing to do the publishing venture with Cooper because he was family. Pete went back to him and said Cooper was going to do it, even though he had no desire to publish outside of his traditional contracts. That was why Pete had to start a company under Cooper's name—so Ron would think he was still working with Cooper, who was publishing under the pseudonym Peter Becker—and Pete could receive the money in Cooper's name.

"After Cooper died, Pete claimed that Mallory was still willing to publish some of Cooper's unpublished novels, with Pete as the go-between. That was why we kept coming across Mallory's name in the investigation, and two of the bank tellers at Mayhew Bank recognized Doreen Beckford and thought her name was Mallory Beck."

"I still can't believe she was impersonating me in my own hometown. That takes courage." I shook my head. "And who is Pirro Klytaimnestra? Is that Pete?"

Alex nodded. "Pete convinced his father that their Greek names were holding them back from having business success in America, but his dad was never going to allow them to officially change their names. They obtained fake IDs under their new names but continued to run their business paperwork through the Klytaimnestra name. That's what first led me to a connection between Pete and Pirro and why I knew he was lying to me when he said he was only staking out the house on Marsh Avenue. I just didn't have quite enough on him to prove that Cooper's accident was actually intentional."

"Cooper was always too trusting and too forgiving. I remember an uncle of his wanting to meet with him just after he got his first book deal, but I had no idea that was Ron Beckford or that he was a criminal mastermind looking for places to launder his money. Did you catch him, too?"

Alex shook his head. "It seems even if Pete had made it to the dock, Ron's boat wouldn't have been there. As soon as Ron got wind of the police in Honeysuckle Grove asking questions, he and his estranged wife, Doreen, got into their boat and haven't been seen since."

"Do you think you'll ever catch him?"

Alex shrugged. "Maybe not me, but I have faith that the law will eventually catch up to Ron Beckford. And now that we have a solid witness giving testimony against him, he and his wife won't have such an easy time getting out of prison." He took another bite, chewed, and then went on. "Apparently, Ron had already run hundreds of thousands of dollars through Pete's publishing venture while Cooper was alive, but the first book wasn't making back enough money, no matter how much advertising he threw at it. Ron was threatening to come after Cooper for the money just as Cooper started asking a lot of questions. Pete claimed that if he didn't take care of things himself, Ron Beckford would have come after Cooper and really made him and probably you suffer."

I shook my head in disbelief. "All this time, I felt in my gut like something didn't add up about Cooper's death, but my dad and my sister, they kept telling me I should just put it out of my mind and move on. Even my new therapist thought I was overreacting."

Amber placed a hand over mine on the table. "I felt the same way with my dad. If I hadn't had you here . . . " It was the most emotion Amber had shown with me, but she couldn't continue it and looked down, shaking her head. When she had composed herself, she met my eyes again. "But at least I had you, believing me when I said something was wrong. That's why you're here in Honeysuckle Grove, you know? I'm sure of it. To help people who no one else will listen to. To help them find closure."

Her words rang true inside me. Maybe that *was* why I'd ended up in Honeysuckle Grove and had chosen to stay, even after Cooper was gone. Realizing I had a purpose here and wasn't simply floundering gave me an immeasurable amount of peace. It wasn't just angst and suspicion or seeking validation that caused my drive to investigate. What Amber said made sense. I cared about people and wanted to help them find peace in their lives, too.

"I think you're right," I said, looking between them. "But I hope you both know I'm not planning on doing that alone."

My best friends smiled back at me. Even Hunter came over and nuzzled his nose under my hand. We had moved from being an unbeatable foursome to a bit of a disgruntled fivesome. I looked over at the sliding glass door where Hunch kept his eyes trained on Alex's new police dog, ready to leap away to safety if any of us came near the door.

This was my family. We would learn to get along—even our animal contingent. And Amber was right. We would keep helping the people of Honeysuckle Grove uncover the truth and find their closure.

It was why we were all here and why we'd stay together indefinitely.

# THE END

# Up Next: Murder in New Orleans...A Mallory Beck Cozy Culinary Novella (Book 8)

\* THIS HUMOROUS, CONTEMPORARY travel mystery was originally published as *Murder of a Po' Boy* in the *When the Cat's Away* Anthology

**A food tour in New Orleans where murder is on the menu...**

When Mallory Beck wins a food tour experience in New Orleans, she invites teenage Amber, her foodie BFF, to join her on a road trip of French and creole cuisine. Mallory's cat-sitter cancels at the last minute, and presumptuous, cheeky Hunch helps himself to shotgun in Mallory's Prius. A good thing, too, because when a know-it-all food tour participant turns up dead and wrapped in Mardi Gras beads, they'll need Hunch's keen nose to sniff out any foul play.

Surrounded by tight-lipped locals and voodoo theories, Mallory and her team of sleuths have their work cut out for them to clear Amber's name from suspicion and get to the bottom of what happened to the Po' Boy who didn't make it through to the last stop on the food tour.

**Order Murder in New Orleans now at  or turn the page to read the first three chapters!**

# Chapter One

I⊤ WAS SIX O'CLOCK in the morning and I was already talking a blue streak to my ornery cat.

"Listen, Hunch, you'll like Seth. I promise. He's related to Amber, so how bad could he be, right?" Using my six-teen-year-old BFF's name made Hunch pause from his pacing along the backseat of my white Prius. In truth, I didn't know much about Amber's older brother, Seth. "You'll have to stay in his room because their mom is allergic to all things furry, but Seth goes out all the time. He'll take you with him."

This was a guess, but apparently, Seth liked animals. I'd at least asked that much.

When I pulled into the driveway of Amber's mom's man-sion, the sun's glow was barely peeking over the horizon. The town felt dark and quiet so I turned off my engine and picked up my phone to text Amber.

**~Should I bring Hunch in or does Seth want to come out and get him?~**

Three dots appeared. I waited a long time for two words to appear.

**~About that...~**

I stared at my phone, but no more dots appeared. Even Hunch sensed something was wrong and climbed onto the console to nuzzle up to my shoulder—a good deal more af-fection than my late husband's cat usually gave me. I didn't believe animals could read, and yet, I clearly wasn't convinced because I flashed him my phone screen so he could have a peek.

He let out a mix between a mewl and a growl.

"I know." I stroked his head, accepting the rare opportunity when he'd let me give him some love. Still, the dots indicating her reply didn't appear. "I have a bad feeling about this, too—"

A knock on the passenger window made me slap a hand to my chest as my heart skipped a beat and then pounded. But it was only Amber. I'd neglected to unlock her door.

She opened the door, but didn't get in. A red and white duffel bag sat at her feet, and she wore a black hoodie that read: THAT'S A HORRIBLE IDEA. WHAT TIME?

I didn't notice her frown until she picked up Hunch and cuddled him to her neck. He immediately started purring.

"Bad news, Hunchie." Amber was the only one who could get away with cutesy nicknames with my cat.

"What? What bad news?" I strained my neck to see the dark upper rooms of the Montrose mansion. "Where's Seth?"

My hope deflated before I even had the question out. I'd been looking forward to this road trip for months. After Amber had entered a cooking contest at school, she'd caught the bug for competition and insisted I enter *Foodie Elite Magazine*'s original recipe contest. The food tour I'd won tickets to in New Orleans had high ratings in all the food magazines, and I'd heard great things even before I won the tickets.

"Seth can't take Hunch?" I guessed because Amber still hadn't answered me.

"Seth can't take Hunch," she echoed into my cat's fur.

Hunch wasn't the type of cat you could drop off at any old pet kennel. Hunch had been my mystery-author-husband's assistant before he passed, and I often suspected the cat had a bigger brain than I did. He wouldn't last a day in a cage without a single stimulating human conversation.

And it would dishonor Cooper's memory to put Hunch in such a place.

I heaved out a sigh, trying to let go of my anticipation for the trip.

"But I came up with a backup plan," Amber said.

I raised an eyebrow in question. With her bristly attitude, she didn't have a lot of school friends, and her mom claimed to be highly allergic. Our detective friend, Alex Martinez, worked twelve-hour days, so he wasn't an option either.

"It turns out our hotel accepts pets." She continued to hide half her face behind Hunch, clearly concerned about my re-action.

"They accept pets? In the hotel rooms?"

Hearing the disbelief in my tone, Amber placed Hunch into the passenger seat and pulled out her phone. She navigated to the sponsoring hotel's website and flashed her screen to show me the words: AND YOU CAN BRING YOUR SMALL PET!

I stared at the words, tentatively allowing a spark of hope. "You want to bring Hunch on a fifteen-hour car ride?" My eyebrow was so high, I was certain it blended with my hairline.

"Why not?" Spoken like a true teenager.

"Why not," I echoed under my breath. But I did have Hunch's litter box and food with me for Seth. Hunch knew better than to scratch up furniture. "You're going to be all by yourself for two days while we're on our food tour," I told my cat in my sternest tone.

This apparently signaled my agreement and made Amber squeal into the quiet early-morning air. She raced to the back of my car to throw her bag into the trunk.

I turned to my cat, who waited patiently on his haunches for Amber in the passenger seat with what could only be described as a look of triumph.

"You win. Apparently, you're coming with us."

# Chapter Two

WITH ALMOST A THOUSAND miles to cover in one day, I didn't have much more energy for arguing, so I caved pretty quickly to Amber's pleas to practice her driving. She needed fifty hours for her level one permit, and we both knew her mother wouldn't help with that.

Soon, Amber had her phone hooked into the sound system, and music was playing. I was surprised it wasn't her usual top-forty fare.

"Jazz?" I asked.

"Uh-huh. I downloaded a whole playlist to get us in the mood."

Amber was like me that way. When she did things, she liked to do them right. With our latest venture—a catering business—she was forever coming up with theme ideas for our menus. "It'll make us memorable," she'd said right from the beginning. And it had. We had quickly gained a following within Honeysuckle Grove.

A road trip to New Orleans, followed up by an elite food tour, should have been exciting enough on its own to be memorable, but with the excitement in our lives lately, from helping our detective friend, Alex, in solving murder cases to quite literally running for our lives, I was happy to let Amber make these next four days memorable for less exciting reasons.

I was back in the driver's seat by the time we made it to our hotel, just after eleven, which was right downtown in the French Quarter and overlooked the Mississippi River. As expected for a Friday night, the city was lively with music and people, and if I hadn't been so exhausted, I might have wanted to go exploring.

"This is where they're putting us up?" Amber asked. "Ritzy."

High praise from a girl who had grown up traveling to five-star hotels with her family.

I felt a little underdressed in jeans and a T-shirt. After I parked, she grabbed her duffel bag from the trunk. I looked from my now-wide-awake cat to the tall tower of hotel rooms, lit along the frame with narrow blue lights.

"You're sure they allow pets?" I suddenly wondered if Amber had stretched the truth or shown me a different hotel's website to get her way.

Amber furrowed her brow, which didn't inspire confidence. "Oh. Yeah. Maybe I'll wait out here with Hunch while you double-check."

"They *don't* allow pets?" After a fifteen-hour drive, I was way too tired for this.

"They have some rooms for pets. Ask if they can move us to one." Amber shrugged, like this wasn't such a big deal.

I sighed out my fatigue and reached for the door.

I had a feeling it wasn't going to be that easy.

# Chapter Three

SURE ENOUGH, THE FRONT desk clerk practically laughed in my face when I asked if my room allowed pets or if they could move me to a room that did.

The fortysomething man shook his head. "We have one theme room designed for small pets but it's always booked up *months* in advance. Why? You don't have a pet with you now?" The alarm was clear in his tone.

"Oh, no, nothing like that." I laughed nervously while wondering when I might have time to find us another pet-friendly hotel. "My niece was thinking of adopting a... dog while we were here in town. But I'll tell her it won't work this trip."

Thankfully, the front desk clerk accepted my explanation and handed over two key cards. I took them and gritted my teeth all the way to the car.

"Nope. No pets in our room," I told Amber the second she got out of the car. "Apparently, there's only *one* room allowing pets and it books up months in advance. Who knew?" Amber loved to dish out sarcasm, so I figured she'd better be able to take it.

She nodded, solemn for only about two seconds. Then she reached inside the car and retrieved Hunch, placing him into her duffel bag.

I pulled my small suitcase from the trunk, which had doubled in weight. "What on earth...?"

"I put some of my stuff in there to make room for Hunch." Amber bent to murmur something to Hunch before covering the opening of the duffel bag with her jacket.

I supposed I should just be happy she had some kind of a plan. My tired brain was ready for a good night's sleep.

Inside the hotel's front doors, we angled for the elevator, but halfway through the small lobby, a tall slender blond man intercepted us.

"Mallory Beck?" he said such a strong Irish accent, it almost sounded put on. I nodded. "Howya? Liam O'Conner, at your service. I'll be your host from Foodie Elite Tour." He held out a hand, and I shook it. "Jerome said you'd pulled up." Liam motioned to the front desk clerk, who was watching us.

On instinct, I angled my body to hide Amber and her duffel bag. "Oh, yes. We couldn't leave West Virginia any earlier, so I'm afraid it was a long day of driving for us." I hoped he'd infer that all I wanted in the world right now was a bed.

But he just laughed heartily. "It's grand. And who's this youngwan with ya?"

I'd been trying to keep the focus away from Amber, so I quickly rattled off, "This is my niece, Amber. Hey, that's a great accent you have. Is it Irish?"

He nodded, but didn't elaborate. "And will you be joining us on the food tour, Amber?"

"Yeah, we're super excited for it, right, *Aunt* Mallory?" She elbowed me. We often posed as aunt and niece while working investigations, but I'd just saddled her with calling me Aunt Mallory for the duration of the two-day tour.

Liam turned toward the bar, which gave me a chance to sidestep a couple of feet away and press the elevator button. But when I turned back, another couple headed our way. "You should meet some of our other guests. We were chatting in the bar. Will you have a mineral with us?"

Was mineral water common in New Orleans? Or perhaps Ireland? Or was it code for some other sort of drink? Didn't matter. I certainly didn't have the energy or the pet-freeness to sit and visit in a bar right now.

"Oh, I'd like to, but—"

"Clive, Scarlett, this here's Mallory and her niece, Amber. They'll be joining us on the tour."

Clive had a sweep of black bangs that appeared shellacked into place. He reached to shake my hand vigorously. "How y'all doin'? Nice of you to bring your niece to this thing. She's gonna learn a lot from me about good food. So are you, I bet." Clive's voice was even louder than Liam's, and I wondered how many "minerals" he'd had tonight.

Scarlett stood back and smiled quietly. She had bright or-angey-red hair and wore a flowered tea-length swing dress, like something out of the fifties. I was about to ask about her gorgeous vintage pendant with tiny pearls draped along the bottom edge when she put in, "Clive knows a lot about food. He studied cooking in Paris."

"That's right." Clive puffed out his chest.

I hadn't been to Paris, but from everything I'd heard, I had trouble picturing loudmouthed immodest Clive studying there.

"Come on! Join us in the bar," Clive said. "Liam's been rattling on about himself for too long."

I had a feeling Clive had been the self-involved talker.

"Ahh, Mallory and Amber are knackered," Liam answered for me. "And I should get some good sleep myself. Going to be a full day tomorrow."

Clive's eyes slid down to Amber's side, where she clutched her duffel.

I stepped into his vision and reached out a hand. "It was so nice to meet you, Clive. I look forward to getting to know you and Scarlett better in the morning."

Thankfully, the three of them let us go. As I looked at Amber's slightly wriggling duffel bag, I wondered if Liam was also staying in the hotel and if he'd be joining us in the elevator. But thankfully, a second later, the elevator dinged its arrival, and Liam stuck around to wish Clive and Scarlett a good night.

"What are we going to do with Hunch while we're on tour?" I slid my key card into the lock of a fancily carved white door. "If we leave him here, the maid will find him."

As I opened the door, Amber pulled the Do Not Disturb sign from the back of it. "We'll just put this up."

Everything seemed so easy for Amber.

"There's no way his litter pan will fit in either your duffel bag or my suitcase. How do you suppose we're going to sneak that up here?" I hoped she had let my cat out on some grass before bringing him upstairs.

She shrugged—her ever-present response to every conundrum. "So we'll bring him in the car."

"In the middle of July?"

"We'll put the sign up, and I'll come back and take him out." She swept by me into our room and effectively changed the subject. "Whoa, Mallory! Look at this room."

She placed her duffel bag on the floor, and Hunch wormed his way out of it. A second later, he was sniffing every inch of our floor.

The Mardi Gras-themed room was decked out in lime green and fuchsia drapes. At the end of our brocaded bedspreads was a row of brightly colored bobbles the size of my head that imitated Mardi Gras beads.

"This is awesome!" Amber spun around and landed on her back on one of the beds, looking up at the chandelier and the masks that decorated the upper half of the room.

It warmed my heart to see her this happy. I didn't think I'd heard her so excited in the entire year I'd known her. At sixteen, she deserved some wonder in her life.

I sighed and dropped onto the other bed.

We'd figure out what to do with Hunch after a good night's sleep. Instead of focusing on what was wrong, I turned to Amber, smiled, and said, "Yes, this is all going to be amazing."

Order Murder in New Orleans now to read the rest!

# Reviews Matter...

HONEST REVIEWS HELP BRING new books to the attention of other readers. If you enjoyed this book, I would be grateful if you would take five minutes to write a couple of sentences about it. You can find all the books in this series to leave reviews at the following link.

http://books2read.com/denisejaden

Thank you so much for your support. I couldn't do this without readers like you!

Turn the page for a recipe from Mallory's Recipe Box...

# From Mallory's Recipe Box – Amber and Mallory's Crepes!

I GREW UP WITH my dad making crepes for the family on weekend mornings. The table would be filled with every kind of topping you could imagine and our family would sit around building our own unique creations.

Below you'll find a simple crepe recipe. Add an extra tablespoon of sugar if you'd like to make dessert crepes, or leave as is for savory varieties.

Below that, you'll find some of our favorite filling combinations to try out on your own.

**INGREDIENTS:**

- 1 cup whole milk

- ¼ cup water

- 2 large eggs

- 2 tablespoons melted butter

- 1/2 tsp granulated sugar (or 2 tablespoons for dessert crepes)

- 1 cup all-purpose flour

- 1/2 teaspoon salt

- additional melted butter, for brushing

# INSTRUCTIONS

1. **BLEND:** In a blender, add liquid ingredients on the bottom for a smoother blend. Blend until the batter is mixed and smooth. Refrigerate for at least 1 hour and up to 48 hours.

2. **CREPES:** Use an electric crepe maker or heat an 8-inch skillet over medium heat. Brush the skillet with melted butter. Lift the skillet with your dominant hand and pour a ¼ cup of the prepared crepe batter into the skillet with the other hand, as you tilt and rotate the pan to spread the batter evenly. The first one may be a little thick in spots. Allow the crepes to cook, about 1 - 2 minutes or until the tops look dry and the edges start to lift up and away from the pan. Flip them. They should be slightly golden with bubbly brown spots. The second side will only take about 30 seconds. Remove to a plate and continue to cook additional crepes, stacking one on top of the other. Crepes can be made a day in advance, stacked, covered with plastic wrap (on a plate) and refrigerated until ready to serve.

Savory Fillings:

1. Cream cheese and smoked salmon

2. Gruyere cheese with prosciutto

3. Scrambled eggs, mushrooms, and feta

4. Chicken and your favorite flavor of Boursin cheese

5. Turkey, avocado, walnuts, and a Dijon vinaigrette

Sweet Fillings:

1.

Cinnamon caramelized apples with vanilla ice cream

2. Nutella with sliced bananas and whipped cream

3. Vanilla yogurt, granola, and sliced fruit

4. Sweet whipped cream and jam

5. Whipped cream, strawberries and sugared lemon zest

Enjoy!

# Join My Cozy Mystery Readers' Newsletter Today!

Would you like to be among the first to hear about new releases and sales, and receive special excerpts and behind-the-scene bonuses?

Sign up now to get your free copy of ***Mystery of the Holiday Hustle – A Mallory Beck Cozy Holiday Mystery***.

You'll also get access to special epilogues to accompany this series—an exclusive bonus for newsletter subscribers. Sign up below and receive your free mystery:

https://www.subscribepage.com/
mysteryreaders

# Acknowledgements

THANK YOU TO MY amazing team of advance readers, brainstormers, and supporters. It's getting to be such a long (and wonderful) list of people, but I am so very thankful for every single one. And to you, Reader: I appreciate you just for picking up this book and giving it a chance!

Thank you to my developmental editor, Louise Bates, my copyeditor, Sara Burgess, my "Strange Facts Expert" Danielle Lucas, my cover designer, Steven Novak, and illustrator, Ethan Heyde.

Thank you for joining me, along with Mallory, Amber, Alex, and Hunch on this journey. We're thrilled to have you along on this ride!

## THE TABITHA CHASE DAYS of the Week Mysteries

Book 1 - Witchy Wednesday

Book 2 - Thrilling Thursday

Book 3 – Frightful Friday

Book 4 – Slippery Saturday

Mystery Anthology (Including Book 5 – Dead-end Week-end)

## The Mallory Beck Cozy Culinary Capers:

Book 1 – Murder at Mile Marker 18

Book 2 – Murder at the Church Picnic

Book 3 – Murder at the Town Hall

Christmas Novella – Mystery of the Holiday Hustle

Book 4 – Murder in the Vineyard

Book 5 – Murder at the Montrose Mansion

Book 6 – Murder during the Antique Auction

Book 7 – Murder in the Secret Cold Case

Book 8 – Murder in New Orleans

Find all the Mallory Beck novels at bit.ly/MalloryBeck!

## Collaborative Works:

Murder on the Boardwalk

Murder on Location

Saving Heart & Home

## Nonfiction for Writers:

Writing with a Heavy Heart

Story Sparks

Fast Fiction

Denise Jaden is the author of the Mallory Beck Cozy Culinary Capers and the Tabitha Chase Days of the Week Mysteries. She is also the author of several critically-acclaimed young adult novels, as well as the author of nonfiction books for writers, including the NaNoWriMo-popular guide Fast Fiction.

In her spare time, Denise acts in TV and movies and dances with a Polynesian dance troupe. She lives just outside Vancouver, British Columbia, with her husband, son, and one very spoiled cat.

Sign up on Denise's website to receive bonus content (you'll find clues in every bonus epilogue!) as well as updates on her new Cozy Mystery Series.

www.denisejaden.com

Made in United States
North Haven, CT
10 March 2023

33856635R00114